What Was Happening?

Her brain wouldn't form thoughts at all, but her mouth had no trouble responding to his.

Heat rushed through Constance to her fingers, which were suddenly on the soft cotton of his shirt. She felt his hands on her back, his touch light and tender. His tongue met hers, sending a jolt of electricity to her toes.

The stubble on his chin scratched her skin slightly as the kiss deepened. His arms wrapped around her, enveloping her in their embrace. She dug her fingers into the roping muscle of his back, plucking at his shirt as their lips moved together.

A humming sound startled them both and they broke the kiss. "My phone," he murmured in a low voice. He didn't reach for it. Still frowning slightly, he raised a thumb and smoothed a strand of hair from her cheek.

She blinked, wondering what had just happened. And why? "I really must..." She wasn't even sure what she really must do. Go to bed? Take a cold shower? Throw herself out the window?

Did he really just kiss her?

* * *

Dear Reader,

There are quite a few romances featuring Native American heroes from the West or the Great Plains, but rarely any from the East Coast. This story takes place in Massachusetts, where my hero, John, has recently gathered the remains of his small tribe, sought formal recognition from the government and jumped all the legislative hurdles required to open a casino. I invented an imaginary tribe inspired by the story of the Mashantucket Pequots, who bounced back from near extinction and created the Foxwoods Casino in Connecticut. Massachusetts may in fact soon have a tribal casino, since the Mashpee Wampanoag—who gained official recognition as a tribe in 2007—are planning to open one in their Cape Cod town.

My heroine, Constance—who thoroughly disapproves of gambling—has been sent to investigate the casino's books, and is disturbed to find herself attracted to its charming and charismatic owner. Can you say "conflict of interest"? I hope you enjoy John and Connie's story.

Best wishes,

Jennifer Lewis

A HIGH STAKES SEDUCTION

JENNIFER LEWIS

ISBN-13: 978-0-373-73347-7

A High Stakes Seduction

This edition published by arrangement with Harlequin Books S.A.

For questions and comments about the quality of this book, please contact us at CustomerService@Harlequin.com.

Printed in U.S.A.

Books by Jennifer Lewis

Harlequin Desire

^*The Prince's Pregnant Bride* #2082
^*At His Majesty's Convenience* #2094
^*Claiming His Royal Heir* #2105
Behind Boardroom Doors #2144
†*The Cinderella Act* #2170
†*The Deeper the Passion...* #2202
†*A Trap So Tender* #2220
Affairs of State #2234
A High Stakes Seduction #2334

Silhouette Desire

The Boss's Demand #1812
Seduced for the Inheritance #1830
Black Sheep Billionaire #1847
Prince of Midtown #1891
Millionaire's Secret Seduction #1925
In the Argentine's Bed #1931
The Heir's Scandalous Affair #1938
The Maverick's Virgin Mistress #1977
The Desert Prince #1993
Bachelor's Bought Bride #2012

*The Hardcastle Progeny
^Royal Rebels
†The Drummond Vow

Other titles by this author available in ebook format.

JENNIFER LEWIS

has been dreaming up stories for as long as she can remember and is thrilled to be able to share them with readers. She has lived on both sides of the Atlantic and worked in media and the arts before she grew bold enough to put pen to paper. She would love to hear from readers at jen@jenlewis.com. Visit her website at www.jenlewis.com.

For Dwnell

Acknowledgments

Many thanks to my editor Charles Griemsman.

One

"Just get rid of her as quickly as possible. She's dangerous."

John Fairweather scowled at his uncle. "You're crazy. Stop thinking everyone's out to get you."

John didn't want to admit it, but he too was rattled by the Bureau of Indian Affairs sending an accountant to snoop through New Dawn's books. He glanced around the grand lobby of the hotel and casino. Smiling staff, gleaming marble floors, paying customers relaxing on big leather couches. There was nothing he didn't love about this place. He knew everything was aboveboard, but still…

"John, you know as well as anyone that the U.S. government is no friend of the Indian."

"*I'm* friendly with them. They gave us tribal recognition. We ran with it and built all this, didn't we? You need to relax, Don. They're just here to do a routine audit."

"You think you're such a big man with your Harvard degree and your Fortune 500 résumé. To them you're just another Indian trying to stick his hand in Uncle Sam's pocket."

Irritation stirred in John's chest. "My hand isn't in anyone's pocket. You're as bad as the damn media. We built this business with a lot of hard work and we have just as much right to profit from it as I did from my software business. Where is she, anyway? I have a meeting with the contractor who's working on my house."

The front door opened and a young girl walked in. John glanced at his watch.

"I bet that's her." His uncle peered at the girl, who was carrying a briefcase.

"Are you kidding me? She doesn't look old enough to vote." Her eyes were hidden behind glasses. She stood in the foyer, looking disoriented.

"Flirt with her." His uncle leaned in and whispered. "Give her some of the old Fairweather charm."

"Are you out of your mind?" He watched as the woman approached the reception desk. The receptionist listened to her, then pointed at him. "Hey, maybe that is her."

"I'm serious. Look at her. She's probably never even kissed a man before," Don hissed. "Flirt with her and get her all flustered. That will scare her off."

"I wish I could scare you off. Get lost. She's coming over here."

Plastering a smile on his face, John walked toward her and extended his hand. "John Fairweather. You must be Constance Allen."

He shook her hand, which was small and soft. Weak handshake. She seemed nervous. "Good afternoon, Mr. Fairweather."

"You can call me John."

She wore a loose-fitting blue summer suit with an ivory blouse. Her hair was pinned up in a bun of some kind. Up close she still looked young and was kind of pretty. "I'm sorry I'm late. I took the wrong exit off the turnpike."

"No worries. Have you been to Massachusetts before?"

"This is my first time."

"Welcome to our state, and to the tribal lands of the Nissequot." Some people thought it was cheesy when he said that, but it always gave him a good feeling. "Would you like something to drink?"

"No! No, thank you." She glanced at the bar, looking horrified, as if he'd just thrust a glass of neat whiskey at her.

"I mean a cup of tea, or a coffee." He smiled. It would to be quite a challenge to put her at ease. "Some of our customers like to drink during the day because they're here for fun and relaxation. Those of us who work here are much more dull and predictable." He noticed with chagrin that his uncle Don was still standing behind him. "Oh, and this is my uncle, Don Fairweather."

She pushed her glasses up on her nose before shoving out her hand. "Pleased to meet you."

Don't be so sure, John wanted to tease. But this was a business meeting. "Let me take you up to the offices, Ms. Allen. Don, could you do me a favor and see if the ballroom is set up for the Shriners' conference tonight?"

His uncle glared at him, but moved off in the right direction. John heaved a sigh of relief. It wasn't always easy working with family, but in the end it was worth the hassle. "Let me take your briefcase. It looks heavy."

"Oh, no. I'm fine." She jerked away as he reached toward her. She was jumpy.

"Don't worry. We don't bite. Well, not much, anyway." Maybe he should flirt with her. She needed someone to loosen her straitjacket.

Now that he'd got a better look at her, he could see she wasn't quite as young as he'd first assumed. She was petite but had a determined expression that showed she took her job—and herself—very seriously. That gave him a perverse urge to ruffle her feathers.

He glanced at her as they headed for the elevators. "Is it okay if I call you Constance?"

She looked doubtful. “Okay.”

“I do hope you’ll enjoy your time at New Dawn, even though you’re here to work. There’s a live show in the Quinnikomuk room at seven and you’re most welcome to come see it.”

“I’m sure I won’t have time.” Mouth pursed, she stood and stared at the elevator doors as they waited.

“And your meals are on the house, of course. Our chef used to work at the Rainbow Room, so our food here is as good as any fancy restaurant in Manhattan.” He loved being able to brag about that. “And you might want to reconsider about the show. Tonight’s performer is Mariah Carey. Tickets have been sold out for months.”

The elevator opened and she rushed in. “You’re very kind, Mr. Fairweather—”

“Please call me John.”

“But I’m here to do my job and it wouldn’t be appropriate for me to enjoy…perks.” She pushed her glasses up her nose again. The way she pursed her lips made him think how funny it would be to kiss them. They were nice lips. Plump and curvy.

“Perks? I’m not trying to bribe you, Constance. I’m just proud of what we’ve built here at New Dawn, and I like to share it with as many people as possible. Is that so wrong?”

“I really don’t have an opinion.”

When they arrived at the floor with the offices, Constance hurried out of the elevator. Something about John Fairweather made her feel *very* uncomfortable. He was a big man, broad shouldered and imposing, and even the large elevator felt oddly small when she was trapped in there with him.

She glanced around the hallway, not sure which way to go. Being late had her flustered. She’d planned to be here half an hour early but she'd taken the wrong exit ramp and gotten lost and—

"This way, Constance." He smiled and held out his hand but withdrew it after she ignored him. She wished he'd turn off the phony charm. His sculpted features and flashing dark eyes had no effect on her.

"How do you like our state so far?"

Again with the charm. He thought he was pretty hot stuff. "I really haven't seen anything but the highway medians, so I'm not too sure."

He laughed. "We'll have to fix that." He opened the door to a large open-plan office space. Four of the five cubicles she could see were empty, and doors stood open to the offices around the walls. "This is the nerve center of the operation."

"Where is everyone?"

"Down on the floor. We all spend time serving the customers. That's the heart of our business. Katy here answers the phones and does all the filing." He introduced her to a pretty brunette in a pink blouse. "You've met Don, who's in charge of promotion and publicity. Stew handles building operations, so he's probably out there fixing something. Rita is in charge of IT and she's in Boston looking at some new servers. I handle all the accounting myself." He smiled at her. "So I can show you the books."

Great. He shot her a warm glance that did something really irritating to her stomach. He was obviously used to having women eat out of his hand. Lucky thing she was immune to that kind of nonsense. "Why don't you hire someone to do the accounts? Aren't you busy being the CEO?"

"I'm CFO and CEO. I take pride in managing all the financial aspects of the business myself. Or maybe I just don't trust anyone else." He flashed even white teeth. "The buck stops here." He tapped the front of his smart suit with a broad finger.

Interesting. She felt as if he'd thrown down a gauntlet and challenged her to find something wrong with the books. She liked that he took personal responsibility.

"It's a family-run business. Many of the people in the office are tribal members. We also outsource to other local businesses—printing, web design, custodial services, that kind of thing. We like to support the whole community."

"Where is the community? I booked a room at the Cozy Suites, which seemed to be the nearest motel, but I didn't see it as I drove up here."

He smiled. "The nearest town is Barnley, but don't worry. We'll set you up in a comfortable room here. We're booked to capacity, but I'm sure the front desk can figure something out."

"I'd really rather stay elsewhere. As I said, it's important to be objective."

"I can't see how where you stay would affect your objectivity." Those dark eyes peered at her. "You don't seem like the type to be swayed by flattery and pampering. I'm sure you're far too principled for that."

"Yes, indeed," she said much too fast. "I'd never let anything affect my judgment."

"And one of the nice things about numbers is that they never lie." He held her gaze. She didn't look away, even though her heart was thudding and her breath getting shallow. Who did he think he was, to stare at her like that?

She finally looked away first, feeling as if she'd lost a skirmish. Never mind, she'd win the war. The numbers themselves might not lie, but the people reporting them certainly could. She'd seen some pretty tricky manipulations since she'd gone into forensic accounting. The BIA had hired her accounting firm, Creighton Waterman, to investigate the New Dawn's books. She was here to make sure the casino was reporting profits and income accurately and that no one had skimmed anything off the top.

She braced herself to meet his gaze again. "I specialize in looking beneath the shiny rows of numbers that companies put in their annual reports. You'd be surprised what turns up when you start digging."

Or would he? She was looking forward to getting her fingers on last year's cash-flow data and comparing it with the printed reports. She wouldn't have time to look at every single number, of course, but she'd soon get a sense of whether there was fudging going on.

"The Nissequot tribe welcomes your scrutiny." His grin did something annoying to her insides again. "I'm confident you'll be satisfied with the results."

He gestured for her to walk into one of the offices. She hurried ahead, half-afraid he was going to usher her in with one of his big hands. The office was large but utilitarian. A big leather chair sat behind the desk, and two more in front of it. A New Dawn wall calendar was the only decoration. Annual report brochures from the last three years sat on the big, polished wood desk, and filing cabinets lined one wall. A round table with four chairs sat in one corner. The realization crept over her that this was his personal office. He pulled open a drawer. "Daily cash register receipts, arranged by date. I add up all the figures myself first thing every morning."

He rested a hand on the most recent annual report, fingers pressing into the shiny cover. Such large hands weren't quite decent. He certainly didn't look like any CFO she'd encountered. All the more reason to be suspicious.

"Make yourself comfortable." He looked at the chair—his chair. She had to brush right past him to get to it, which made her skin hum and prickle with an unpleasant sensation. Worse yet, he pulled up another chair and sat down right next to her. He opened the most recent brochure, which had a picture of a spreading oak tree on the cover, and pointed at the profit data at the top of the first page. "You'll see we're not kidding around here at New Dawn."

Forty-one million in net profits was no joke, for sure. "I've seen the annual reports already. It's really the raw data I'm interested in."

He pulled out a laptop from the desk drawer and punched up a few pages. "The passwords change weekly, so I'll keep you posted, but this account information will get you right into our daily operation. You should be able to look up and analyze any data you need."

Her eyes widened as he clicked through a few screens and she saw he was letting her peek right at the daily intake and outflow.

Of course the numbers could be fudged. But she was impressed by how quickly he could click from screen to screen with those big fingers. They were large enough to hit two keys at once. Was he wearing cologne? Maybe it was just deodorant. His scent kept creeping into her nose. His dark gray suit did nothing to conceal the masculine bulk of his body, which was all the more evident now that he was sitting only inches from her.

"These documents here are monthly reports I do of all our activities. If anything unusual happened, I make a note of it."

"How do you mean, unusual?" It was a relief to distract herself from noticing the tiny dark hairs dusted across the back of his powerful hands.

"Someone winning a suspiciously large amount. Anyone who gets banned, complaints from the public or from staff. I believe in paying close attention to the small details so the big ones don't take you by surprise."

"That sounds sensible." She smiled. Why? She had no idea.

Just being professional. Or so she hoped. He'd smiled at her, flashing those dazzling white teeth, and her face had just mirrored his without her permission.

She stiffened. This man knew he was having an effect on her. "Why do you produce annual reports when you're not a public company?"

"I don't answer to investors like a public company, but I have a greater responsibility. I answer to the Nissequot people."

From what she'd read on the internet, the Nissequot tribe was mostly his immediate family, and the entire reservation was a creative interpretation of local history for the sole purpose of pursuing a very profitable business venture. "How many of you are there?"

"We've got two hundred people living here now. A few years ago, there were only four of us. In five years' time I'm hoping we'll number in the thousands." There was that smile again.

She jerked her eyes back to the screen. "It probably isn't too hard to persuade people to come when you're offering a cut of forty-one million dollars."

His silence made her look up. He was staring right at her with those penetrating eyes. "We don't give individuals any handouts. We encourage tribal members to come here to live and work. Any profits are held in trust for the entire tribe and fund community initiatives."

"I'm sorry if I offended you." She swallowed. "I didn't mean to." She felt flustered. The last thing she wanted to do was put him on the defensive.

"I'm not offended at all." He didn't smile, but looked at her pleasantly. "And maybe we could build the tribe faster if we just handed out checks, but I'd rather attract people more slowly and organically because they want to be here."

"Quite understandable." She tried to smile. She wasn't sure it was convincing. Something about John Fairweather rattled her. He was so...handsome. She wasn't used to being around men like him. The guys in her office were mostly introverted and out of shape from sitting hunched over their computers all day long. John Fairweather obviously spent a good amount of time at his desk, judging from all the material he'd showed her, but somehow—tan and sturdy as the oak tree on the cover of his annual report—he looked more like someone who spent all day outdoors.

"Are you okay?"

She jerked herself out of the train of irrelevant thoughts. "Maybe a cup of tea would be a good idea, after all."

Constance lay in her bed at the Cozy Suites Motel, staring at the outline of the still ceiling fan in the dark. Her brain wouldn't settle down enough for sleep but she knew she needed to rest so she could focus on all those numbers at the casino tomorrow. She wanted to impress her boss so she could ask for a raise and put a down payment on a house. It was time to move out from under her parents' wing.

It was one thing to move back home to save money after college. It was another entirely to still be there six years later, when she was earning a decent salary and could afford to go out on her own. Part of it was that she needed to meet a man. If she was in a normal relationship with a nice, sensible man, a practiced charmer like John Fairweather would have no effect on her, no matter how broad his shoulders were.

Her parents thought almost everyone on earth was a sinner who should be shunned. You'd think she'd told them she was planning to gamble all her savings away at the craps tables the way they'd reacted when she announced she was going to Massachusetts to look into the books of a casino. She'd tried to explain that it was a big honor to be chosen by her firm to undertake an important assignment from a government agency. They'd simply reiterated all their old cautions about consorting with evildoers and reminded her that she could have a perfectly good job at the family hardware store.

She didn't want to spend her life mixing paint. She tried to be a good daughter, but she was smart and wanted to make the most of what natural talents she had. If that meant traveling across state lines and consorting with a few sinners, then so be it.

Besides, she was here to root out wrongdoing at the casino. She was the good guy in this situation. She shifted onto her side, trying to block out the thin green light from the alarm clock on the bedside table. If only she could get her brain to switch off. Or at least quiet down.

A high-pitched alarm made her jump and sit up in bed. Something in the ceiling started to flash, almost blinding her. She groped for the switch on her bedside light but couldn't find it. The shrieking sound tore at her nerves.

What's going on? She managed to find her glasses, then climbed out of bed and groped her way to the wall light switch, only to discover that it didn't work. The digital display on the clock radio numbers had gone out.

A jet of water strafed her, making her gasp and splutter. The overhead sprinkler. A fire? She ran for the door, then she realized that she needed her briefcase with her laptop and wallet in it. She'd just managed to find it by the closet, feeling her way through the unfamiliar space illuminated only by the intermittent blasts of light from the alarm, when she smelled smoke.

Adrenaline snapping through her, Constance grabbed her briefcase and ran for the door. The chain was on and it took her a few agonizing seconds to get it free. Out on the second-floor walkway of the motel, she could see other guests emerging from their rooms into the night. Smoke billowed out of an open door two rooms away.

She'd forgotten to bring shoes. Or any clothes. She was more or less decent in her pajamas, but she could hardly go anywhere like this. Should she go back in and get some? Someone behind her coughed as the night breeze carried thick black smoke through the air. She could hear a child crying inside a room nearby.

On instinct she yelled, "Fire!" and—clutching her briefcase to her chest—ran along the corridor away from the fire, pounding on each door and telling the people to get out. Had someone called the fire department? More people were coming out of their rooms now. She helped a family with three small children get their toddlers down the stairs to the ground floor. Was everyone safe?

She heard someone calling 911. She rushed back up the stairs to help an elderly couple who were struggling to find their footing in the smoky darkness. Then she ran along the corridor and banged on any doors that were still closed. What if people were still in there? She hoped that the sirens and lights would have flushed everyone out by now, but…

A surge of relief swept over her as she saw fire engines pull into the parking lot. It wasn't long before the firemen had finished evacuating the building and moved everyone to the far end of the parking lot. They trained their hoses on the fire, but whenever the flames and smoke died down in one area, they sprang up in another.

"It's a tinderbox," muttered a man standing behind her. "All that carpet and curtains and bedspreads. Deadly toxic smoke, too."

Soon the entire motel complex—about twenty rooms—was ablaze and they had to move farther back to escape the heat and smoke. Constance and the other guests stood there in their pajamas, watching in stunned disbelief.

At some point she realized she'd put her briefcase down while helping people out, and she had no idea where it was. It had her almost-new laptop in it, her phone and all the notes she'd made in preparation for her assignment. Most of the information was backed up somewhere, but putting it all back together would be a nightmare. And her wallet with her driver's license and credit cards! She started to wander around in the darkness, scanning the wet ground for it.

"You can't go there, miss. Too dangerous."

"But my bag. It has all my important documents in it that I need for work." Her voice sounded whiny and pathetic as she scanned the tarmac of the parking lot. The fire glowed along almost the entire roof of the motel, and acrid smoke stung her nostrils. What if she didn't find her bag? Or if it got soaked through?

"Constance."

She jerked her gaze up and realized John Fairweather was standing in front of her. "What are you doing here?"

"I'm a volunteer firefighter. Are you cold? We have some blankets on the truck."

"I'm fine." She fought the urge to glance down at her pajamas. How embarrassing for him to see her in them, though it was pretty selfish and shallow of her to be thinking about how she looked at a time like this. "Is there anything I can do to help?"

"You could try to calm down the other guests. Tell them

we'll find room for everyone at the New Dawn hotel. My uncle Don's driving over here in a van to pick everyone up."

"Oh. That's great." She'd made quite a fuss about not staying there. Now apparently she would be anyway.

"Are you sure you're okay? You look kind of dazed. Maybe you should be treated for smoke inhalation." His concerned gaze raked over her face. "Come sit down over here."

"I'm fine! Really. I was one of the first ones out. I'll go talk to people." She realized she was flapping her hands around.

John hesitated for a moment, then nodded and hurried off to help someone unfurl a hose. She stood staring after him for a moment. His white T-shirt shone in the flashing lights from the fire trucks, accentuating his broad shoulders.

Constance Allen, there is something very, very wrong with you that you are noticing John Fairweather's physique at a moment like this. She picked her way barefoot over the wet and gritty tarmac to where the other guests stood in a confused straggle. One little girl was crying, and an older lady was shivering even under a blanket. She explained that a local hotel had offered them all rooms and that a bus would be coming to fetch anyone who couldn't drive there.

People realized they'd left their car keys locked in their rooms, and that started a rumbling about everything else they'd lost and only intensified Constance's own anxiety about her briefcase and all her clothes, including a nice new suit she'd just bought. She tried to soothe them with platitudes. At least no one was hurt. That was a big thing to be grateful for.

Still, she didn't have her car keys, either. If she'd flown

here and rented the car she could have just called the rental agency. But she'd decided to be adventurous and driven her own car all the way here, so now she couldn't even get into it. She was starting to feel teary and pathetic when she felt a hand on her arm.

"I found your bag. You left it at the bottom of the stairs." John Fairweather stood beside her, holding her briefcase, which dripped water onto the tarmac.

She gasped and took it from his hand, then noticed with joy that it was still sealed shut. "You shouldn't have gone back over there." The fire was now out, but the balcony and stairs were badly damaged and collapsing.

John's T-shirt was streaked with soot. "You shouldn't have brought it with you. We firefighters hate it when people retrieve stuff before escaping."

"My…my laptop." She clutched the handle tightly. Tears really threatened now that she had her bag back. "It has everything on it."

"Don't worry, I'm just teasing you. I'd have a hard time leaving my laptop behind even after all the training I've had." His warm smile soothed the panic and embarrassment that churned inside her. She felt his big hand on her back. "Let's get you back to the hotel."

Her skin heated under his unwelcome touch, but she didn't want to be ungracious after he'd found her bag and offered her a place to stay. The flashing lights from the fire trucks hurt her eyes. "My car keys are gone."

"We'll get you another set tomorrow. I'll drive you back in my car." His broad hand still on her back, he guided her through the crowd toward his vehicle. *Oh, dear.* Even amid all the chaos, her skin heated beneath his palm as if she was still too close to the flames.

And now she was going to be trapped in his glitzy hotel in nothing but her pajamas.

Two

"We were lucky the motel had a good fire alarm system." John steered his big black truck down a winding back road. "It went up fast. Everyone got out, though."

"That's a relief. I'm glad the firefighters got there quickly and had time to check all the rooms. How long have you been a volunteer?"

"Oh, I joined the first moment they let me." He turned and grinned. "More than fifteen years ago now. When I was a kid I wanted to be a firefighter."

He should have become one. Much better than a gambling impresario. On the other hand, her strict upbringing had formed her distaste for gambling, but now that she was here it didn't seem so different from any other business. She admired how John had pitched in and done anything and everything he could to help. He was thoughtful, too, talking to the other evacuees and reassuring them that the hotel staff would help them track down car keys, clothes and things like that in the morning. There was certainly no need for him to have offered everyone rooms at the hotel. He was being very generous. "What changed your mind?"

He shrugged. "I discovered I had a head for business. And at the time I was glad to leave this quiet backwater behind. I got seduced by the bright lights of the big city."

"New York?"

"Boston. I've never lived outside of the great state of Massachusetts. After a while, though, I started to miss the old homestead. And that's around the time I cooked up the whole casino idea. But when I came back I signed right on with the fire department again." His disarming grin cracked her defenses again. "They missed me. No one can unfurl or roll up a hose as fast as me."

"I'm sure they appreciate the help. But there don't seem to be too many people around here." They were driving through dark woods, not a house in sight. The area around the casino was very rural.

"Nope. That doesn't seem to stop fires breaking out, though. Last week an abandoned barn caught fire out in the middle of nowhere. We had to pump water from an old ice pond to put it out. Could have set the whole woods on fire, especially right now when everything's so dry."

It was early summer. Not that she really noticed the changing seasons much from the inside of her pale gray cubicle.

As they continued driving, she could see the pearl-white moon flashing through black tree branches. The woods were beautiful at night.

"I think it's nice that you find the time to volunteer when you're so busy with the casino." There. She'd said it. She'd been a little short with him this afternoon and now she felt bad about it.

"I enjoy it. I'd go crazy sitting behind a desk all the time. I like to have my hands on as many things as possible."

One of those hands was resting on the wheel. For one breath-quickening instant she imagined it resting on her thigh.

She crossed her legs and jerked her gaze back to the moon, only to find it had disappeared behind the trees altogether. What was wrong with her? His hand was filthy from fighting the fire, for one thing. And she would rather die than let a business client touch her.

Not that he'd want to anyway. She'd seen the gossip-column pictures of him with all those glamorous women. A different one every week, from the looks of it. He'd hardly be interested in a frumpy accountant from Cleveland.

She let out a sharp exhale, then realized it was audible.

"Fires are stressful, but don't worry too much. Everything you lost can be replaced. That's the thing to remember."

She turned to him, startled. She hadn't even given a thought to all her burned-up stuff. Clearly she was losing her mind. "You're so right. They were just things."

They drove in silence for a minute.

"It's a shame you missed Mariah Carey. She was awesome." He turned and smiled.

"I'm sure she was." She couldn't help smiling back. Which was getting really annoying.

"What kind of music do you like?"

"I don't really listen to music." She shifted in her seat. Why did they have to talk about her?

"None?" She felt his curious gaze on her. "There must be some kind of music you like."

She shrugged. "My dad didn't allow most music in the house."

"Now that's a crime. Not even gospel music?"

"No. He thought singing was a waste of time." She frowned. Gaining maturity had given her a perspective on her father's views that made living in the house difficult. What was wrong with a little music? He thought even classical music was an enticement to sin and debauchery. Sometimes her friend Lynn drove them both to lunch and they listened to the radio on the way. She was surprised by how some tunes made her want to tap her toes.

She noticed with relief that they were pulling into the casino parking lot.

"So what did your family do for fun?"

Fun? They didn't believe in fun. "We didn't have too much time on our hands. They run a hardware store, so there's always something to do."

"I guess organizing rivets made accounting seem like an exciting escape." He grinned at her.

She bristled with irritation, then realized he was right. "I suppose it did." He pulled into a parking space in front of New Dawn, then jumped out of the car and managed to open her door before she even got her seat belt undone. There was no way to avoid taking his offered hand without being rude, and she didn't want to be obnoxious since he was going out of his way to help her. But when she did, his palm pressed hotly against hers and made all kinds of weird sensations scatter through her body.

Get a grip on yourself! Mercifully he let go of her hand as they paused at a back door to the hotel block and he unlocked it with a key. She was grateful not to have to walk through the glittering lobby in her pj's.

Then he put his arm around her shoulders.

Her skin tingled and heated through the thin fabric of her pajama top. What was he thinking? He was talking and she really couldn't hear a word. He probably thought this was a warm and encouraging gesture for someone who'd been through a traumatic experience. He couldn't have any idea that she hadn't had a man's arm around her in years and that the feeling of it was doing something very unsettling to her emotions.

His arm was big and heavy. He was so much taller than she that he simply draped it casually across her shoulders as if he was resting it. Then he squeezed her shoulders gently.

"Right?"

"What?" She had no idea what he'd just asked.

"You still seem kind of dazed, Constance. Are you sure you didn't get concussed or something?" He paused and pulled his arm from around her shoulders so he could peer into her eyes. "You look all right, but these things can sneak up on you. Maybe we should call for the nurse. We have one on staff here, to look after any guests who need attention." They were standing next to an elevator and he pressed the button.

"I'm fine, really! Just tired." She spoke a bit too loudly, then peered imploringly up at the digital display, only to find that the elevator was three floors away.

"No problem." He pulled a phone from his pocket and made a call. "Hi, Ramon. Is six seventy-five ready yet?" He nodded, then winked at her. *Winked?* It was probably just some friendly indication that the room was indeed ready. Her social skills were rather limited, since she only interacted with accountants. Still, it made her heart start racing as if she'd run a marathon.

She didn't know why, either. Yes, he was handsome. Tall, dark, all the usual stuff. But right now she was tired and stressed out and if she was anywhere near as dirty as he was she must look very unattractive, so he certainly wasn't flirting with her.

The elevator doors opened and she darted in and pressed the button for six. He strolled in after her. She focused her gaze on the numbers over the door as the elevator rose. He didn't say a word, but his very presence seemed to hum. There was something…unnerving about him, something that made her hyperaware of his presence.

When the elevator doors opened, she leaped out and

glanced about, trying to figure out which way to go. She jumped slightly when she felt his fingers in the hollow of her back.

"This way." He guided her down the hallway. She walked as fast as she could and his fingers fell away, which made her sigh with relief. He didn't mean anything by it; he probably didn't even notice he was touching her. He was one of those overly friendly types who hugged everyone—she'd noticed that after the fire. All she had to do was get into her room, shower, get some sleep and she could deal with everything else in the morning.

He pulled a key card from his pocket and unlocked the door. The spacious hotel room beckoned her like an oasis—crisp white sheets, closed ivory curtains, soothing art with images of the countryside. "This looks amazing."

"I'll need to get your clothes from you so we can wash them."

She glanced down. Her pj's were smudged with soot. "I'm going to need some real clothes for tomorrow."

"What size are you? I'll have one of the girls find something for you."

She swallowed. Telling John Fairweather her dress size seemed dangerously intimate. "I think I'm a six." And what would he tell them to buy? "Something conservative, please. And I'll pay for it, of course."

He grinned. "Did you think I'd ask them to pick out something racy?"

"No, of course not." Her cheeks heated. "You don't know me well, that's all."

"I'm getting to know you. And I'm getting to like you, too. You stayed calm during the fire and were very helpful. You'd be surprised how many people lose their heads."

She fought a burst of pride. "I'm a calm person. Very dull, in fact."

His dark eyes peered into hers. "Don't sell yourself short. I'm sure you're not dull at all."

Her mouth formed a silent *oh.* Silence—and something bigger—lingered in the air. Panic flickered in her chest. "I'd better get some sleep. I have a headache." The lie would probably give her a forked tongue, but she was on edge and John Fairweather was not helping her sanity.

"Of course. You can leave your clothes outside the door. There's a laundry bag in the closet."

"Great." She managed a polite smile, or was it a grimace? Her body sagged with relief as his big, broad-shouldered presence disappeared through the door and it closed quietly behind him.

Constance showered and washed her hair with rose-scented shampoo. The luxurious marble bathroom was well stocked with everything she needed, including a comb and a blow-dryer. She dressed in the soft terry robe with *New Dawn* embroidered in turquoise on the pocket. She'd put her dirty pajamas in a laundry bag outside the door for the hotel staff to pick up. Her briefcase had mercifully kept her laptop and important papers dry, so she'd emptied it and put it on a luggage rack to dry out. There was nothing more she could do for now. Hopefully she could relax enough to get some sleep.

But as soon as she laid her head on the cool, soft pillow, she heard a knock on the door. She sat up. "Coming." It was very late for someone to knock. Maybe the hotel staff had a question about the bag she'd left outside the door. Or maybe they'd already found her something to wear tomorrow?

She took the latch off the door and opened it a crack… to reveal the large bulk of John Fairweather blocking the light from the hallway.

"I brought you some aspirin." He held up a glass, then opened his other palm to reveal a tiny sachet of some painkiller that actually wasn't aspirin at all.

"Oh." She'd forgotten about her "headache." With considerable reluctance, she opened the door wider. "That's very kind of you." She took the pills from his hand, making sure not to touch him.

"And I brought you some clothes from the gift shop downstairs. It's lucky we're open twenty-four hours." She noticed a shiny bag under his arm.

"Thanks." She reached out for it, only to find that he'd already walked past her into the room. She shook her head and tried not to smile. He wasn't shy, that's for sure. Of course, it was his hotel.

"Did you find everything you need?" He put the bag down on the desk and turned to her with his hands on his hips. "It's not too late for room service. There's someone in the kitchen all night."

"Thanks, but I'm not hungry."

John had also showered and changed. He wore dark athletic pants and a clean white T-shirt that had creases as if it was right out of the package, except that the creases were now being stretched out by the thick muscles of his broad chest. His dark hair was wet and slicked back, emphasizing his bold features and those penetrating eyes.

She blinked and headed for the shopping bag. Before she got there, he picked up the bag and reached into it himself. He pulled out a blue wrap dress with long sleeves. It looked like something she'd wear to a cocktail party. "We don't really have office attire in the guest shop."

"It's lovely and very kind of you to bring it." *Now please leave.*

"And we found some sandals that almost match." He pulled out a pair of dark blue glittery sandals and looked at her with a wry grin. "Not exactly the right look for the office, but better than being barefoot, right?"

She had to laugh. "My boss would have a heart attack."

"We won't tell him."

"It's a her."

"We won't tell her, either." He looked at her for a moment, eyes twinkling, then frowned slightly. "You look totally different with your hair down."

Her hands flew to her hair. At least she'd blow-dried it. "I know. I don't ever wear it down."

"Why not? It's pretty. You're pretty."

She blinked. This was totally unprofessional. Of course, nothing about this situation was professional. She was standing here in her bathrobe—in his bathrobe—in his hotel that she'd explicitly said she wouldn't stay in. And now he was giving her gratuitous compliments? "Thanks."

She felt that stupid smile creeping over her mouth again. Why did this man have such an effect on her? *Think about computational volatility in Excel spreadsheets. Imagine him cheating on his taxes. Imagine him...*

Her imagination failed her as his mouth lowered hotly over hers.

Heat rushed through her, to her fingers, which were suddenly on the soft cotton of his T-shirt. She felt his hands on her back, his touch light and tender. His tongue met hers, sending a jolt of electricity to her toes. *Oh, goodness.* What was happening? Her brain wouldn't form thoughts at all, but her mouth had no trouble responding to his.

The stubble on his chin scratched her skin slightly as the kiss deepened. His arms wrapped around her, enveloping her in their embrace. As her chest bumped against his, her nipples were pressed into the rough texture of the bathrobe and sensation crashed through her. She dug her fingers into the roping muscle of his back, plucking at his T-shirt as their mouths moved together.

A humming sound startled them both and they broke the kiss. "My phone," he murmured, low. He didn't reach for it. Still frowning slightly, he raised a thumb and smoothed a strand of hair from Constance's cheek.

She blinked, wondering what had just happened. And why? "I really must…" She wasn't even sure what she really must do. Go to bed? Take a cold shower? Throw herself out the window? Heat darted through her body, and she didn't know how much longer her knees would hold her up without his strong arms around her.

"Take your aspirin. I'll see you in the morning." He hesitated, phone still vibrating in his pocket. An expression of confusion crossed his face and he shoved a hand through his wet hair. "I'll call a local dealership about replacing your car keys first thing."

"Thanks." The word was barely audible, but it was a miracle she managed to force it out at all. He walked backward a couple of steps, gaze still riveted on hers, before he nodded a goodbye and strode to the door.

As it slid quietly shut behind him, she stood there, mouth open, knees still trembling. Had he really just kissed her? It didn't seem possible. Maybe she'd imagined it. In fact, maybe she'd dreamed up this whole crazy scenario while sleeping fitfully in her lumpy bed at the Cozy Suites Motel. A fire and a kiss in one night? Impossible.

She pinched herself and it hurt. That wasn't good. Maybe she *should* throw herself out the window. A desire to gulp in cool night air made her hurry to it, but it was one of those big modern ones that didn't open.

Probably a good thing. She looked out and could see nothing but dark woods barely illuminated by a cloud-shrouded moon.

She'd grabbed him, fisting her hands into his T-shirt, and clawed at his back. Had she totally lost her mind? Her breath came in heaving gasps and blood pounded in her veins.

It had been a very long time since she'd kissed anybody. Since anyone had kissed her, or even shown the slightest interest in doing so. Her one and only boyfriend, Phil, had broken up with her right before they graduated from college. Four years together, sustained by promises of marriage and family and happily ever after, and he'd simply told her that he wasn't ready and he was moving to Seattle without her. Her parents would die—or they'd kill her, or both—if they knew she'd given Phil her virginity outside the sanctity of marriage. They'd blame her for throwing herself away and point out that of course he wouldn't want to marry a woman like that.

The pain and shame of it all was achingly fresh even after six years, so she tried not to think about it.

And now something like this? She could taste John's lips on hers, his tongue winding with hers, and the memory made her heart pulse harder. She couldn't even blame him. She couldn't swear that he'd even started the kiss. It had just happened. And it had happened all over her body, which now hummed and throbbed with all kinds of unfamiliar and disturbing sensations.

She'd lost her clothes, her car keys and now her mind. How would she ever get to sleep now?

Three

"Thanks for picking everyone up last night, Don." John leaned back in his chair in the hotel restaurant and brushed croissant crumbs from his fingers. "I know I interrupted your hot date."

"Anything for you, John. You know that." His uncle sipped his coffee. "Though why you feel the need to help a bunch of total strangers, I don't entirely know."

John shrugged. "Nowhere else for them to go. And Constance Allen was with them." His lips hummed slightly at the sense memory of their kiss. He hadn't planned it, and the chemistry between them had taken him by surprise.

Don put his cup down with a bang. "What? I didn't see her."

"I brought her in my car." He schooled his face into a neutral expression.

"So she's here, right now, in the hotel?" His uncle's eyes widened. "And you didn't even tell me?"

John sipped his coffee. "I'm telling you right now."

Don's long, narrow mouth hitched into a half smile. "Did you put a move on her?"

"Me?" He raised a brow noncommittally. He didn't want to give Don the satisfaction of knowing. And he hadn't kissed her to please anyone but himself.

Don laughed and slapped his hand on the table. "You

kill me. I bet she'll look like a startled rabbit today. Heck, she looked like one yesterday."

John frowned. "You need to stop making assumptions about people, Don. I'm sure she has a lot of dimensions you know nothing about. At the fire last night, for example, she kept her cool and was very helpful. Nothing like a startled rabbit."

Don cocked his head. "If I had half the charm you do I'd never be lonely again."

"You're not lonely all that much now, from what I can see."

"The money from this place doesn't hurt." His uncle laughed. "I was lonely a lot before. I didn't have the knack for making bank that you were born with."

"It's not a knack. It's called hard work." He kept checking the door, waiting for Constance to show up.

"All the hard work in the world doesn't help if you aren't lucky." Don took a bite of his eggs. "Luck is our bread and butter."

"You make your own luck." John scanned the dining room. Had he missed her coming down? He wanted to see her. "Statistics are our bread and butter. Anyone dumb enough to rely on luck will lose it all to the house sooner or later."

"Unless they know how to game the system."

"Impossible." John drained his coffee. "I personally make sure it's impossible. I'm going up to the office. Don't forget to send out the press release about the new lineup of shows. I want press coverage."

"I know, I know. Who booked them all?"

"You did. And Mariah Carey was amazing last night."

Don grinned. "I love my job."

"Me, too." John slapped Don on the back as he headed out of the dining room. His uncle could be a pain in the ass, but underneath all the bluster he had a good heart and put a lot into making the entertainment here as much of a draw as the gaming tables.

But where was Constance? She wasn't in his office. He'd tried calling her hotel room, but no one picked up. He didn't want to knock on her door again. That hadn't gone entirely as planned last time.

He strolled across the lobby.

"You seen Constance Allen?" The staff at the front desk shook their heads. He would have to go up to her room again. He took the elevator to the sixth floor, excitement rippling in his veins. Why had she let him kiss her? In retrospect, it surprised him. She'd seemed so uptight and buttoned-down, but she'd opened like a flower and kissed him back with passion.

He couldn't wait to see what would happen this morning. Of course he probably shouldn't be entertaining lustful thoughts about the accountant investigating their books for the BIA. On the other hand he knew she wouldn't find anything wrong, so what did it really matter? No one would ever know but the two of them.

He knocked on the door. "It's John."

He heard some rustling, and cracked his knuckles while waiting. The door opened a crack and a pair of bright hazel eyes peered out at him.

"Good morning." A smile spread across his mouth. Chemistry crackled in the air again. Which was odd, really, because by any objective standards he wouldn't have thought they'd be a match. Maybe it was that opposites-attract thing.

And she was pretty.

"Um, hello." The door didn't open any farther.

"Can I come in?"

"I don't think that's a good idea." He saw her purse her pretty pink lips.

"I promise I won't try anything," he whispered. "In fact I'm not sure what happened last night, and if an apology is in order then I offer one." Not that he was sorry.

The door still didn't budge. Now she was biting that sensual lower lip. Which had an unfortunate effect on his libido.

"I called the dealership about your car. They're going to program a new key and bring it over here before noon."

"That's great. Thanks."

"Don't you want to come up to the office and look through the books?"

She blinked rapidly. "Yes. Yes, I do."

"All right then. I won't come in. You come out instead."

The door closed for a moment and he heard some rattling, then she appeared again, carrying her bag. "I just had to get my laptop." She opened the door and stepped out into the hallway, looking self-conscious—and very lovely—in the blue dress he'd found for her. He wasn't sure whether to compliment her or not, and decided not to. He didn't want to make her feel any more uncomfortable.

Her hair was fastened back up into a tight bun that showed off her pretty neck. As usual she wore no makeup, and the freshness of her clear skin was heightened this morning by an endearing flush of pink on her cheeks.

"I hope you managed to get some sleep after all the excitement of last night."

Her pace quickened as she headed down the hall toward the elevator. He'd meant the fire, but he realized she'd thought he meant the kiss. The memory of it flashed through his brain, firing all kinds of inappropriate impulses.

"I slept fine, thank you." Her words were clipped and

terse. "I'd like to look at the receipts from your first two years of operation this morning."

"Of course." The temptation to touch her was overwhelming. Normally he'd probably have done it without even realizing, but everything about her energy warned him to back off. "Have you had breakfast?"

"Perhaps I could grab a roll or something from the dining room before I head up to your office."

"No need. I'll have some food brought up." He reached for his phone. "Tea or coffee?"

"Neither, thanks. A glass of water would be fine."

He sneaked a glance at her as she pressed the elevator button. Shoulders tense and bag clutched in her hand, she looked as if she might explode. She probably didn't want to risk ingesting stimulants. He could think of a few ways to help her relax, but none of them was appropriate in the circumstances.

Maybe later, though.

As they got on the elevator, he told one of the new kids who was interning for the summer to bring some eggs and toast and fruit up to the office. And a roll. And some juice and water. But even as he concentrated on ordering the food, he noticed how the enclosed space of the elevator felt strangely tight this morning, the atmosphere abuzz with…something.

He followed her off the elevator, admiring the way she carried herself as she walked across the floor to his office. Then she stopped and frowned slightly.

He gestured for her to open the door. "Head in and make yourself comfortable."

"Is there another office I can work in? I don't want to inconvenience you."

"The only way you could inconvenience me is by making me carry all the files out of my office and into another one." He shot her a glance. "So you'll do me a favor by working in here. I have things to do anyway, so I won't be around much." He hoped that would put her at ease.

She put her bag down on the round table in the corner. "When did you say my car keys would be ready?"

"Noon. And I'll drive you over there to retrieve it."

"Again, I don't want to put you to any inconvenience. Is there someone less…important who can drive me?" She was avoiding his glance as she moved toward his desk.

"We're all important here. It's how we run the place. Every Nissequot has a crucial role to play and would be missed as much if not more than me. The cashiers will be hustling today, as we're expecting twenty buses of retirees visiting from Cape Cod this morning."

"Oh." Her brow wrinkled slightly as she reached for the pile of folders she'd pulled the day before. She bumped her elbow on a jar of pens, accidentally scattering them across the desk. He grabbed one just before it flew over the edge.

Their fingertips brushed as he handed it back to her. Her hand flinched away as though she'd been stung. Somehow that only increased the tension snapping in the air.

He shouldn't have kissed her. She was here on business and was obviously very reserved and proper. She wasn't looking to get her hands on him.

Quite the opposite.

Was that why he'd been irresistibly drawn to her? Was it the challenge of the seemingly unobtainable? There was something more, though. An energy that drew him to her. Something deep and primal. And when she'd folded into his arms and melted into the kiss…

John turned his attention to the filing cabinet with the receipts she wanted. Something had happened between them and he didn't know why. Unplanned and inappropriate, it had stirred his blood and left him wanting more.

Just get rid of her as quickly as possible. His uncle's words simmered in his brain. Sensible advice, under the circumstances. The way her movements snapped with precision and anxiety right now—fingers tapping on her keyboard and eyes darting across the rows of numbers on the papers she'd pulled from the files—she was rushing to get out of here.

So it was all good, right?

John frowned. Was he really the player the Massachusetts press made him out to be? Maybe he was. "Let me know if there's anything I can do for you." The innuendo wasn't entirely intentional, but he enjoyed her hot-under-the-collar reaction. Shifting in her chair and fussing with her bag, she seemed tense enough to burst into flames.

He'd be happy to help put out the fire. "The food should be here any minute, but maybe I'd better get you some water right now."

"Just some peace and quiet will be fine, please," she muttered, without looking up. She pushed her glasses up on her nose with a fingertip. He noticed she wasn't wearing nail polish.

A smile sneaked across his mouth. He liked that she wasn't afraid to be rude. A lot of people were intimidated by him, especially now that the millions were rolling in. It was refreshing to find someone who treated him as though he was a regular guy. "I'll make myself scarce."

"Good." She still didn't look up.

He chuckled as he removed himself from his own office. He could still taste that kiss on his lips. Constance had a surprising well of passion beneath her prim exterior, and he looked forward to tapping it again—whether or not that was a good idea.

Constance couldn't wait to get her car back. Right now, sitting in the grand lobby of the hotel, she felt like a prisoner in John's luxurious den of vice. Dressed in a silky garment she'd never have chosen, surrounded by people laughing and talking too loud and drinking before it was even lunchtime, she felt totally out of her element.

Maybe her family was right and she should have tried to refuse this job. On the other hand, building a career depended on taking assignments that would enhance her profile in the company, and a contract from a big government agency was a feather in her cap. Luckily New Dawn's files were well organized and the information straightforward, so she'd probably get her work done and be out of here within a week.

She heard her phone chime and fished it out of her bag. The display revealed that it was Nicola Moore, her contact at the Bureau of Indian Affairs.

"Hello, Nicola. I'm sitting in the lobby of the casino right now." She glanced about, hoping the woman wouldn't ask a lot of probing questions that would be embarrassing to answer right here.

"Excellent. Are they allowing you access to the books?"

"Oh yes, Mr. Fairweather—" even saying his name made her blush "—has given me carte blanche to go through all the files in his office. He has the original cash register receipts for every day since the casino opened."

"Do they seem legitimate?"

"The receipts?" She glanced around, hoping no one could overhear their conversation. "They do. So far everything looks good."

There was a pause at the other end. "They think it's a routine audit, but the reason we sent you is that we have good reason to suspect fraud. They may be giving you falsified documents."

Constance bristled. "I have considerable experience in examining retail operations. I know the warning signs, and rest assured I will closely examine anything that looks at all suspicious."

"John Fairweather has a reputation for charming everyone. Don't be fooled by his suave manner—he's a very sharp and cunning businessman."

Constance fumbled and almost dropped her phone. Could Nicola Moore somehow know that John had…seduced her last night? Impossible, surely! "I'm aware of his reputation," she whispered. Where was he? She felt as if he was going to materialize beside her at any minute. "I am completely immune to charm and focused entirely on the numbers." At least she certainly planned to boost her immunity to his charms from now on. That kiss last night had caught her completely by surprise, when she was overwrought and exhausted and emotional from the evening's turmoil.

"Excellent. I look forward to hearing an interim report. The New Dawn has attracted a lot of negative attention since it opened. You may have read some of the commentary in the press. We've been hearing plenty of whispers about their operation. No one can figure out how they managed to open without taking on massive debt, or how they're operating with such impressive profits. It doesn't match the other models we've seen. Frankly, we're assuming that something untoward is going on. Those numbers just can't be real."

Constance frowned. She didn't like that Ms. Moore already assumed a crime was in progress. She'd been surprised by the negative slant of some newspaper articles she'd read about the Nissequot and the New Dawn, too. John and the tribe seemed to attract the kind of backbiting usually reserved for successful celebrities. So far she hadn't seen any evidence of wrongdoing at all. Of course it was only her second day, but still…. John seemed to be a concerned and thorough businessman and she was beginning to get annoyed by the relentless negativity about his success.

Not that she had any interest at all in defending him, of course. That would be highly unprofessional. She prided herself on complete objectivity. But maybe everyone should be a bit more open-minded about the New Dawn's management.

She tensed as she saw John striding across the lobby toward her. You'd think an expensive suit would conceal the raw masculinity of his body, but it didn't. Something about the way he moved made her pulse quicken and her brain start scrambling. Ridiculous! She was far above this kind of girlish reaction. She muttered quickly into the phone that she'd report back as soon as she found anything. Guilt made her fingers tremble as she ended the call.

She stood and clutched her bag to her chest. "Ready?" Her voice sounded a little too perky.

"Yup. A rep from the dealership has dropped off the new key, so you'll be a free woman again in no time."

She smiled and carefully took the key he dangled from his fingers, without letting her skin touch his. "Thank goodness."

"You're welcome to stay at the hotel, of course. There really isn't anywhere else that's convenient. The Holiday Inn is at least twenty minutes away, and that's with no traffic."

"That will be fine." Her words sounded clipped. Thank goodness there was another hotel! Staying here had proven to be an even worse idea than she'd suspected. Hopefully they could both forget completely about that insane lapse of judgment last night and get back to business.

His gaze hovered over her mouth for a moment, and her lips parted. She sucked in a hasty breath. "Let's go."

"Of course." He held out his arm.

She ignored it, gripping her bag tighter.

He pulled his arm back with a rueful glance. Was he really flirting with her? He must be doing it to toy with her. She wasn't stupid enough to think that a man like John Fairweather could actually be attracted to and interested in her. It must be a game for him, to see if he could get the prim little accountant all hot under the collar.

She'd rather die than let him know how well it was working.

In the front seat of his big sedan she pressed her knees together and forced herself to focus on the road ahead. Nothing good could come of watching his big hand on the manual gearshift, or noticing the subtle shift in his powerful thigh muscles as he pressed his foot on the pedals.

"What a beautiful day. I can't believe I lived in the city for so long and didn't even think about what I was missing." His low voice rumbled inside the car.

Constance tugged her gaze from the smooth surface of the blacktop and tried to appreciate nature. Trees crowded the road on both sides, filtering the sun. "How come it's all wooded? Why aren't there farms, or, well, anything?"

"Around the turn of the last century, this was all farmland, but it wasn't close enough to the cities or fertile enough to be profitable, so it was all abandoned. So far suburbia hasn't reached out here, either. If it wasn't for the new highway exit, we'd still be in the middle of nowhere."

"But you grew up here?"

"Yup." He smiled.

She squeezed her knees tighter together. It was just a smile, for crying out loud. No need to get all excited.

"I couldn't wait to get away. I thought this was the dullest place on earth. We had fifty dairy cows and I had to help milk them every morning and evening. Makes tabulating columns of figures look really interesting, let me tell you."

"You've got to be kidding." She couldn't imagine him milking a cow. "I thought that was all done by machines these days."

"It is. But someone has to hook them up to the machines."

"Do they mind? The cows, I mean."

"On the whole they're pretty enthusiastic about it. I guess it feels good to lighten the load."

"And now you milk people foolish enough to gamble their hard-earned money." She looked straight ahead. "You help lighten their heavy wallets."

He turned and looked at her. "You think what we do is wrong, don't you?"

"I'm hardly unusual in that."

"It's entertainment. People have free will. They can come and gamble or they can go do something else."

His calm response only prodded her to goad him more. "Do you gamble?"

He didn't say anything. Silence hummed in the air until she got curious enough to turn and look at him. "No. I don't."

"See?"

"See what?"

"You're smart enough to know it's a bad idea."

"I'm smart enough to know it's not for me. Believe me, it's already a gamble opening a big casino and hotel in the backwoods of Massachusetts when it seems like the whole world wants you to fail."

"I notice that you get a lot of negative press. But I don't suppose it hurts that much, considering the money you're making."

"You're right about that." He shot her another warm

smile that made her toes tingle. She cursed them. "So far we've proved everyone wrong and I intend to make sure it stays that way."

"Why does the BIA want to investigate your accounts?" Was she allowed to ask that? She wanted to hear what he thought.

He shrugged. "Same thing, I think. If we were deeply in debt to a bank in Dubai or the mob, or asking for a government bailout, no one would be surprised. They can't accept that fact that we're successful and prospering all by ourselves. It makes people suspicious."

"Why didn't you need to borrow money?" There probably would have been no shortage of offers. Everyone wanted a piece of this juicy new pie.

"I prefer to be in charge of my own destiny. I sold my software company for eighty million dollars. I'm sure you read about that."

"Yes, but why would you risk your personal fortune?"

"It's an investment, and so far it's worked out fine." She managed not to turn and look at him, but she could see his satisfied smile in her mind. It was really annoying how likable he was. And he didn't gamble? She was having a hard time finding reasons to hate him. And if he wasn't cheating, it made her job harder, because it sounded as if her contact at the BIA wouldn't be happy until Constance found something.

She'd expected them to return to the burned-out motel, but instead he pulled into a restaurant parking lot. Her white Toyota Camry sat off to one side, sparkling clean.

"I had them wash it and bring it here. I didn't think you'd want to see the wreck of the motel. It's a mess over there."

"That was thoughtful." She sneaked a glance at him but

he was getting out of the car, not paying attention to her. "But why did they bring it here instead of the New Dawn?"

Unused to the sandals, Constance stepped out onto what felt like shaky ground. At least now that she had her car back, she could go buy some more sensible clothes and book a room somewhere else. This time she might ask some pointed questions about fire safety. She didn't know what would have happened if the motel hadn't been equipped with alarms.

"I made us a reservation for lunch here."

"What?" She glanced at the restaurant, which—with hanging baskets of lush flowers and elegant striped awnings—looked upscale and expensive. "No! I couldn't possibly. I need to go buy some…toiletries, and clothes. And I want to get more work done back at the office today."

The last thing she needed was to sit opposite John Fairweather over a delicious meal. She'd surely lose the last shreds of her sanity. And really, he had quite a nerve even suggesting it. She should report his behavior to her BIA contact.

Except maybe she'd leave out the part about the kiss.

She climbed into her car and put her bag on the seat next to her. The new key started the engine perfectly, and the brakes screeched slightly as she reversed out of her space too fast. She turned and headed for the exit. It wasn't until she saw John—in the rearview mirror—staring after her that she realized how rude she'd just been.

He was smiling slightly, as if he found the situation funny.

Which made her speed away even faster.

Safely ensconced at the desk in her new room at the Holiday Inn, Constance called her boss's office to let her know why she'd had to move, and ended up speaking to her friend Lynn, the office receptionist.

"It's a bummer that you live with your parents. I wonder if you can claim the loss on their homeowner's insurance."

"I doubt they have any. Their insurance is faith in God. Even if they did, filing a claim would raise the premium."

"If the motel doesn't offer compensation you could sue."

"I'd never do that."

"You're too much like your parents. Living in the wrong century."

"I happen to like this century."

Lynn laughed. "Okay, okay. So how is it going with John Fairweather? Is he as gorgeous as he looks on the internet?"

Constance shifted in her chair. "I don't know what you're talking about."

"I know you like to pretend you're a nun, but I'm sure you can tell whether a man is good-looking or not."

"He's okay looking, I guess." That stupid smile inched across her lips again. Thank goodness no one was here to see it.

"So, how old is he?"

"Early thirties, maybe?"

"That's not too old for you."

"Lynn! What on earth would make you think he and I have anything in common?" They didn't. Nothing. She'd thought about it on the drive over here.

"You're both human. Both single. And you're very pretty, Constance, though you do your best to hide it."

"Would you stop?" She pushed her glasses up her nose. Was she really pretty enough to attract the interest of John Fairweather? It didn't seem possible.

"I'm just excited that you're away from your parents'

overly watchful and critical gaze. You need to make the most of it."

"I've been quite busy getting burned out of my motel room and trying to go through the New Dawn's paperwork."

"All work and no play makes—"

"I'm already dull, and quite happy that way." At least she had been until last night. Suddenly her mind kept churning with odd ideas. That kiss had started something. She kept thinking about it. Feeling his lips on hers. Feeling his arms around her.

Obviously she had to make sure that didn't happen again, but she could kiss someone else, couldn't she? "Maybe I should join one of those dating services when I get back."

"What!" Lynn's stunned response showed that she'd revealed way too much. Now she couldn't even remember how she'd led up to that. "You're finally coming to your senses? It's him, isn't it? Those smoldering dark eyes. Those powerful broad shoulders. I know you're far too principled to be attracted to his money, so it must be his looks."

"Nonsense. He's very intelligent. Nice, too." She froze, realizing that she'd just proved that she liked him.

Silence greeted her on the other end. "Really?" said Lynn slowly.

"Well, I don't know. I only met him yesterday. He's probably just being polite so I won't delve too far into his books."

"I wouldn't blame him. I shouldn't be kidding around like this, though. He does have a reputation as a lothario. I want you to spread your wings, but don't fly right into a fox's den."

"One minute you're encouraging me and the next you're

telling me to back off. It's lucky I have no interest in anything except the books here."

"I can't believe I suddenly feel like I have to warn you off having an affair with John Fairweather."

"I can't believe it, either." *And I also can't believe how much I need warning off!* "Obviously you've forgotten that I'm the same Constance Allen who's only ever dated one man."

"Well, as soon as you get home I'm going to make sure you start dating someone new. When do you get back here, anyway?"

"It'll probably take a week or so. The BIA said I can request more time if I need it. It all depends on what I find."

"I hope you find something. That's always good for business."

"You're actually hoping that a crime is in progress?" Constance's gut clenched at the possibility. "I'm hoping that everything checks out fine. Then I can get out of here as soon as possible." And preserve what was left of her dignity.

Four

She picked up a couple of suits and blouses and a pair of shoes at a local Macy's. It was nearly four by the time she made it back to New Dawn to go over the books. Her eyes darted about, on high alert for any signs of John Fairweather. But she didn't see his imposing form anywhere. He wasn't in the lobby or the elevator. Or leaning over someone's cubicle on the office floor.

He also wasn't in his office, where she sat at the round table, which was inconveniently at coffee table height, and resumed her journey through the files. Where was he? He might be angry that she'd blown him off at lunch. Still, he needed to realize that she was here to do a job, and they'd already spent way too much time together. It would probably be more appropriate to the situation if they weren't interacting at all. On the other hand, her BIA contact had said that often the best information came during an inadvertent slip in casual conversation, so she should spend as much time as possible with the tribal members.

She shook her head. This whole situation was far too confusing for her. Just the fact that Lynn could encourage her one minute and warn her off the next proved that nothing about it made sense. She'd rather be surrounded by quiet and predictable columns of figures.

Which, supposedly, she was right now. Unfortunately

the atmosphere vibrated with the absence of John Fairweather.

Constance stayed until seven-thirty and pored over the files he'd shown her and plenty he hadn't. Nothing aroused her suspicion. If anything, John's accounting methods were somewhat redundant and labor-intensive, and could benefit from some streamlining and a software upgrade.

Relief mingled with disappointment as she descended to the lobby without encountering him. Apparently he'd already forgotten about her and moved on to new pastures. He was probably out on the town right now with some willowy model.

She strode through the lobby, challenging herself not to look around for him. Why did she want to see him? All he did was get her flustered. As Lynn had pointed out, he was a notorious playboy and Constance was peering behind the curtains of his successful operation.

Still, it had been nice of him to personally bring her to the hotel last night, and to pick up her car this morning. On the other hand, if he had her car moved, why hadn't they brought it right to the hotel instead of to some expensive restaurant, where he had apparently intended to continue his inappropriate seduction?

She made her way through the parking lot to her car, brain spinning. Was she upset that he wasn't here to flirt with her and harass her? She should be appalled and disgusted—and suspicious—of his attempts to seduce her. Red flags stuck out of this mess in every direction. Her career at Creighton Waterman would be ruined, and she could lose her accounting credentials, if anyone learned about that kiss. Yet she'd as much as told Lynn that she was attracted to John.

Now she was thinking about him as John?

What was happening to her?

* * *

The next morning she arrived early enough to be the first person in the offices. She'd just settled into browsing through some figures, when John's deep, melodious "Good morning" made her jump. Which was ridiculous since she sat in his office.

"Hello, Mr. Fairweather." She said it as primly as possible. She didn't want him to have any idea of what he'd been doing to her in her dreams last night.

"Mr. Fairweather? Don't you think we're a little beyond that? In fact, I was thinking I should call you Connie."

She blinked rapidly. "No one calls me Connie."

"All the more reason." He sat down on the opposite side of the round table. "What's your nickname?"

"I don't have one."

"I don't believe you." He leaned back. "What do your folks call you?"

"Constance. It's what they named me, so I guess they like it. What do yours call you?"

"John." His eyes twinkled. "So you do have a point. You look great this morning. Did you finally get some sleep?"

Constance felt heat rising to her cheeks. "I did, thank you. The Holiday Inn is very nice."

"I'm sure it is." He cocked his head. "Shame about the twenty-minute drive."

"I don't mind." Why was she getting flustered?

"I'll try not to take it personally."

Of course she was getting flustered. He was staring right at her and flirting.

She watched as he rose from the chair, bowed slightly and left the room. She stared after him, through the open door. Part of her wanted to slam the door and sag against it; another much less reliable part of her wanted to run after him and call, "But wait!"

She closed the door quietly, but resisted turning the lock. As soon as she sat down again, her phone rang and she jumped as if she'd been stung. It was Nicola Moore from the BIA, according to the display. She answered it with as much professional dignity as she could manage.

"Hello, Constance. How are things?"

"Fine. Everything's fine."

"I heard about the fire. I hope that hasn't shaken you up too much."

"It was a shock, but luckily there was no loss of life." She kept quiet about John's role in helping at the fire. There was no need for Nicola to know how much time they'd spent together.

"Have you had a chance to get to know some of the key players yet?"

She hesitated. She wanted to say, *I'm an accountant. I'm better with numbers than people,* but she knew that would be unprofessional. "Sure, I've spoken with several."

"Don't be afraid to get a feel for their personal business. That can often be the most revealing information."

"Uh, sure." Her response wasn't too professional. Still, the request seemed odd. Maybe she just wasn't familiar enough with this kind of work. She knew the BIA regularly conducted audits of various Indian ventures, so they must know what they were doing. "I'll do my best."

She frowned as she hung up. John had done a pretty good job keeping her safely sequestered in his office and away from people. Maybe it was a good idea to move around and take a look at the numbers from the casino floor. There was no reason she couldn't observe the tellers in action, taking people's hard-earned money. It might help stir up her righteous indignation, which seemed to have cooled a bit. She needed to remind herself what this whole enterprise was all about. From an early age, she'd been taught that gambling was wrong, and she still didn't like it much.

She shoved the cap on her pen and put away the latest files she'd looked at. All predictably clean and tidy and all columns adding up to the right amounts. Maybe she was taking John's operation too much at face value. Time to get out there and look under the hood. Feeling like an intrepid reporter, she lifted her bag and headed for the door. She scanned the floor quickly to make sure John wasn't around. Nope. Just two employees sitting quietly at their computers, so she headed downstairs.

She approached the area where the cashiers sat with some trepidation. They were behind a barrier, like at a train station, but it was decorated to look more like an elegant bar than a check-cashing joint. To gain entrance she'd have to go in through the back, and she wasn't sure if they'd let her.

She opened a door marked "staff only," rather surprised that it wasn't locked.

"Can I help you?" A pretty girl with long, curly black hair stood in the hallway behind the door.

"My name's Constance Allen, I'm—"

The girl thrust her hand out. "I know exactly who you are. John told us you might want to see back here. I'm Cecily Dawson. Come in." She smiled, though Constance saw a hint of suspicion in her eyes. Hardly surprising under the circumstances.

"Is it okay if I watch the cashiers for a while?"

"Sure, follow me." She led Constance into the large room, where all the cashiers sat along one wall facing out. Cecily beckoned to a dark-skinned man standing behind the row of cashiers, tapping something into his phone. "Darius, this is Constance Allen."

He pocketed his phone and walked toward her. "A pleasure to meet you, Constance. John told us all about you." His handshake was firm and authoritative. He held her gaze, and her hand, with confidence. He was almost as dangerously handsome as John.

"Is there somewhere I can sit down, out of the way?"

"No need to be out of the way." He touched her arm, and she stifled the urge to flinch. "Come stand with me and watch the whole operation."

"Darius manages the cashiers. He's always on the look-out for trouble."

"In whatever form it may arrive." He shot her a dark gaze filled with mischief.

Constance blinked. "I don't want to get in your way."

"If you're in my way, I'll move." His half smile contained a hint of suggestion. He was flirting with her, too? Maybe this was part of their shtick at the casino. Constance was beginning to regret coming down here. "Each cash register records a sale in our central system and all the records are checked four times a day against the takings. I watch the customers to see if anyone's acting suspicious. It's my job to look for cracks in the system, too, so let me know if you think we could improve upon anything."

"Do you get a lot of suspicious activity?"

"Not so far. We have a lot of controls in place to prevent employees from getting tempted to put their hand in the till. That's more of a problem than the customers at some casinos."

"Are you all members of the Nissequot tribe?"

"Cecily and I are, and Brianna at the end." He pointed to a blonde girl counting out cash at high speed. "Frank, Tessa and Marie are just hoping to marry into the tribe one day." He grinned when Marie, a middle-aged woman in a conservative suit, turned to blow him a kiss. "But we're one big happy family."

His phone beeped and he checked the screen. "Our fearless leader is heading this way," he said to the cashiers. "Look like you're working." He winked at her.

Constance pretended she hadn't seen it. And now John was coming? She braced herself. The cashiers dispensed money with warm customer service and brisk efficiency. They joked and seemed to be enjoying themselves. It wasn't like this at Creighton Waterman. Joviality was frowned upon. In fact, one junior accountant, Daniel Bono, had recently been let go for smiling too much in meetings, or at least that was the rumor.

Customers were streaming into the casino, which struck Constance as a little odd since it was a Wednesday morning. "Why are so many people here at this time of day?"

"We have tour buses pick them up in Boston, Worcester, Springfield. We're adding more routes all the time. A lot of our customers are retirees. We run a brisk trade at the nursing homes."

"Should the elderly be gambling with their life savings?" She felt her brow rise.

Darius's wicked smile reappeared. "Maybe their heirs don't think so, but it's their money, right?"

She shook her head. "I don't get why people want to do this."

"It's fun. Like buying a lottery ticket."

"Do you gamble?"

He shook his head. "John discourages us from gambling. He thinks it's better to put your money in the bank. As far as I know, Don Fairweather is the only gambler in the family. Have you met him?"

"I have. He seems like quite a character."

"I heartily agree."

John burst into the room at that moment. His piercing gaze zeroed in on her. "I was looking for you."

"Now you've found me." She tilted her chin up, proud that she managed to sound so calm. "I was just observing how the cashiers work."

"I see you've met my cousin Darius. He only graduated from college two years ago and he's turning into my right-hand man."

Darius smiled. "I've learned everything from the best."

John put his arm around Darius. "He moved here all the way from L.A. to join the tribe. We're working on the rest of his branch of the family."

"They're not quite ready to move into the backwoods." Darius shrugged. "But the way things are going, this won't be the backwoods for long."

John looked at Constance for a moment. "I'd like to show you around some more."

"I think I've seen everything there is to see. I came through the gaming rooms and passed the slot machines on my way over here."

"Not just the casino and hotel. The whole reservation."

She felt herself frown. Was he trying to shunt her away from here for some reason? She'd barely had time to observe anything. Suspicion crept over her.

On the other hand, she had a feeling Nicola Moore would want her to see as much of the place as possible. "Okay."

"Excellent. We'll start with the museum. Darius can tell you what a passion of mine that has become."

Darius nodded. "It's a labor of love, all right. And thousands of hours of expert research."

"It's not easy to uncover history that's been deliberately buried. Let's go." John gestured toward the door, and she went ahead of him, nodding and smiling to the other employees, and grateful that John hadn't tried to take her hand or put his arm around her.

They walked back through the gaming rooms to the lobby. Retirees were busy wasting their savings in the slot machines, and a surprisingly large number of other people were hunched over the tables as well.

"I didn't know you had a museum."

"There's a lot you don't know." He smiled mysteriously. "All of it good, of course."

"If you're covering up a fraud, you're doing it very well."

"I take pride in everything I do." He lifted a brow slightly, taunting her.

"Are you trying to make me suspicious?" She was conscious of matching his stride as they strolled out of the gaming room and across the lobby.

"Nothing could be further from my mind." Then he touched her. Her stomach drew in and her pulse quickened as he rested his hand at the base of her spine and ushered her though a doorway she'd never noticed before, marked "Hall of Heritage."

It led into a large, gallery-like room with polished wood floors and high walls. Glass cases held artifacts and sleek, printed text and pictures decorated the walls. "It looks like a real museum." She walked ahead of him, curious. One of the first exhibits was a glass case containing a sheaf of age-tinted pages and a quill pen. There was a blown-up photograph of the front page on the wall next to it.

"That's the original treaty between the Nissequot and the governor of Massachusetts in 1648. Two thousand acres of land was given to us then."

"Two thousand? I thought the reservation was less than two hundred."

"They chipped away at it bit by bit over the years."

"The state?"

He shook his head. "Mostly private individuals, farmers, businessmen, greedy people."

"Your ancestors must have sold it to them."

"I could say that greedy people come in all creeds and colors, but research has taught me to give my ancestors the benefit of the doubt and respect that they were just trying to survive."

"You can't really fault them for that. Apparently they managed." She smiled at him. The museum didn't have that many items, but they were carefully arranged and displayed with a good deal of written information accompanying them. A long green cloak in one case caught her eye. It didn't have feathers or beading, but an embroidered trim in black brocade.

"Not what you'd expect, is it?" He looked at her curiously.

"I don't know what I'd expect."

"People seem to want baskets and moccasins and old pots. Precontact stuff. They forget that the history of the Nissequot continues after the settlers arrived. That cloak was worn by Sachem John Fairweather, the man I was named after, when he opened the doors to the first free school in this part of Massachusetts. It remained open until 1933, when the last pupil dropped out to look for work during the Depression."

"Is the building still there?" She could see a grainy photograph of six people in Victorian-era clothing standing outside a neat white building.

"It is indeed. I'm restoring it along with my grandparents' old farmhouse."

"That's very cool. I have no idea of my own family's history before my grandparents' generation."

"Why not?"

She shrugged. "I don't suppose any of us thought it was that interesting."

"Where is your family from, originally?"

"I don't know. All over, I suppose. Maybe that's the problem. It's easy to get excited about ancestry when it's all from one place with a distinct culture. If one person's from Poland and another from Scotland and another from Italy or Norway, no one really cares."

"Well, the truth is that the Nissequot are from all over the place, at this point. I don't even know who my own father was. The Fairweathers are my mother's family. Sometimes you just have to pick a common thread and go with it, and that's what we're doing here. We did find an eighteenth-century Bible with the New Testament written out phonetically in the Nissequot language, though. That's our biggest coup so far. A scholar at Harvard is putting together a Nissequot dictionary by comparing it with a contemporary English version."

She looked up at an enlarged line drawing of a man and woman in more traditional-looking dress. "Is that how you imagine your ancestors looked?"

"Nope. That's a real drawing done by the daughter of one of the first governors of Massachusetts in her personal journal. It was found by relentless digging through old records and hoping for the best. It's time-consuming and way outside my realm of expertise, but it's all coming together piece by piece."

"Impressive."

He led her through the gallery, then disarmed the emergency exit with a key code and pushed through an exterior door out into the bright sunlight. A large black truck was parked right behind the building. "My unofficial vehicle. Get in."

"Where are we going?"

"To meet my grandparents." Curious, she climbed in. His truck wasn't quite as pristine as his sedan. He lifted a pile of papers off the passenger seat so she could sit down. There was an unopened can of soda in the cup holder, and music—the Doors—started as soon as he turned on the engine. There was also a Native American–looking thing with feathers on it hanging from the rearview mirror. "They're going to like you. I can tell."

"Why?" They were hardly likely to appreciate someone who was there for the express purpose of digging up dirt on their reservation.

"You're nice."

"Nice? I'm not nice at all."

His loud laugh echoed through the cab. "True, it was cold of you to blow me off at lunch yesterday. But they'll think you're nice."

She glanced at her reflection in the wing mirror nearest to her. She wasn't sure anyone had accused her of being nice before. Organized, efficient, polite, helpful, exacting, prim, persnickety…a range of flattering and not so flattering words sprang to mind, but nice was not among them. "I'm not sure that nice is good in my line of work."

"Maybe you're in the wrong line of work?" He shot her a challenging glance.

"Look who's talking."

"I'm nice." He glanced in the rearview mirror, then over at her. She jerked her eyes from his gaze and stared out the window, taking in how they were traveling along another featureless wooded road to nowhere. "Ask anyone."

"I'm not sure that's the first word that would spring to mind if I asked someone to describe you. I'd think *bull-headed, relentless* and *determined* would be right up there. And that's just going from the newspaper articles I read about you."

"Don't believe everything you read in the papers."

"I don't, but where there's smoke, there's usually fire." That was one of the first tenets of forensic accounting. The tricky part was finding a live ember after someone had carefully tried to put the fire out.

"They do say I'm an arrogant SOB. I'm guessing you'd agree with that." She saw the corner of his mouth lift in a smile.

"For sure." She felt her own treacherous mouth smile along. "And they say you cooked up the entire Nissequot tribe just so you could open a casino and rake in billions."

"That's pretty much true." He turned and stared right at her. "At least that's how it started, but it's snowballed into a lot more than that."

"Don't you think it's wrong to exploit your heritage for profit?"

"Nope." He looked straight ahead as they turned off one winding road onto another. "My ancestors survived war, smallpox, racism and more than four hundred years of being treated like second-class citizens. Hell, they weren't even American citizens until 1924. The powers that be did everything they could to grind us out of existence and they very nearly succeeded. I don't feel at all bad about taking advantage of the system that tried to destroy us." His voice was cool as usual, but she could hear the passion beneath his calm demeanor. "If I can do something to lift up the people who've survived, then I feel pretty damn good about it."

Constance had no idea what to say as they pulled up in front of a neat yellow neocolonial house with a front porch and a three-car garage.

John had jumped out of the car and opened her door before she managed to gather her thoughts. "What're you waiting for?"

"Uh, I don't know." She'd never felt more lost for words around anyone. "Is this the original farmhouse?" she asked, taking advantage of his offered hand as she climbed down from the cab.

"Oh, no. We just built this three years ago. The old place was kind of a wreck. No insulation, no real heat and A/C. My grandparents were ready to move into someplace shiny and new."

The front door opened and a white-haired man appeared on the front porch. "Hey, Big John."

"His name is John as well?"

"Yes." They walked up the slate front path.

"Does that make you Little John?"

He smiled. "I suppose it does. But if you call me that I won't be responsible for my actions."

She wanted to laugh. As they climbed the steps she could see that the younger John towered over his grandfather by at least eight inches and was fifty-plus pounds heavier, all of it solid muscle.

"This is Constance. She's come here all the way from Ohio to be a thorn in my side."

Big John stuck out a gnarled hand. "Pleased to meet you, Constance." He shook her hand with warmth, using both hands to embrace it. "It's not easy to be a thorn in this man's side. His hide is too tough. Come in."

She followed him into a sunlit foyer, where they were greeted by a tall, rather beautiful woman of about seventy. "This is my mom, Phyllis. She's actually my grandmother, but she raised me so I've always called her Mom."

"Hello, Constance." She also had a firm handshake. Constance could see where John got his inquisitive gaze. She thought it was cute that he called her Mom. "It's not often that John brings a young lady to visit us." Her bright eyes scanned Constance from head to toe.

"Oh, I'm actually not…" Not what? A young lady? She glanced nervously at John.

"Not what?" he said unhelpfully.

"I'm here on business." She glanced from his grandmother to his grandfather. "For the Bureau of Indian Affairs."

"Is that so," said Big John. His expression hardened. She was beginning to get the impression that the BIA was not a much-loved organization.

"I was just showing her our museum. Since she's interested in Indian affairs and all." Constance saw a smile tugging at the corner of John's mouth. "Then I thought she should meet the real reasons we're all here. My mother died when I was young," he told her, "and my grandparents brought me up to be aware of our Nissequot roots. I have to admit that when my friends played cowboys and Indians I wanted to be a cowboy so I could have the gun." He smiled mischievously. "And I wasn't all that interested in hearing stories about how the world was created on the back of a turtle."

His grandfather laughed. "He just wanted to know if the Nissequot liked to fight."

"But they stubbornly persisted in teaching me everything they knew, and it must have taken root somewhere under my thick hide, because I remembered it all."

"How did you know the legends yourselves? Are they all written down somewhere?" Constance couldn't help her curiosity.

"Some stories are. Others are recited or sung," replied Phyllis. "As long as there's one person in each generation left to pass the stories along, they don't die out. Even the family members who've come back to us from places like Chicago and L.A. knew something about their heritage—a song their grandmother used to sing, or just that they were from the Nissequot tribe, even though no one else had ever heard of it. We're so blessed to have John. He's the kind of leader needed to bring the tribe back from near extinction and make it flourish again."

"And there I thought I was just trying to make a buck." He winked at Constance.

"The spirit moves in mysterious ways," said his grandfather. "Sometimes none of us are sure what we're doing until we can look back later. We thought we were trying to run a dairy operation, but we were really keeping our claim on the land going until John was ready to take over."

"John bought us eight cows last Christmas as a present." Phyllis smiled at him.

"Beef cattle," John cut in. "Aberdeen Angus. No more milking." He shrugged. "The place didn't feel right with no cattle on it."

"He missed the sound they make."

"They're an investment. Good breeding stock."

Phyllis smiled at Constance. "He's a lot more sentimental than he'd have you believe."

John huffed. "Nonsense. We'd better get going. I wanted Constance to see that we're not just numbers on a balance sheet or names on a census."

"It was nice to meet you." Constance smiled and waved goodbye, then followed John, who was already halfway out the door. His grandparents stood looking after them, amusement glowing on their faces. He bounded down the front steps and jumped back into the car. The engine was already running by the time she maneuvered herself into her seat.

"They seem very nice."

"Like me." He winked.

"I have to admit that you do seem nicer than all the media stories make you out to be."

"I told you not to believe everything you read. Don't start thinking I'm a pushover, though. I'm as ruthless as I need to be." He tilted his stony jaw as if to prove it.

"Ruthless, huh?"

He focused his dark eyes on her as they paused at the end of the driveway. A shiver of arousal jolted her and she remembered the alarming power he had over her. "Merciless."

John Fairweather knew exactly what he was doing at every moment. Including when he'd kissed her. And she'd better not forget that.

Five

That afternoon, back in John's office, Constance focused on expenses and other outgoings. Expenses were large, as would be expected, and there were definitely some extravagances, but nothing she hadn't seen at other booming corporations.

Around six o'clock she emerged from John's office, ready to head for her hotel. She was relieved that she could be done here in a day or two. Everything was checking out and she and John would no doubt both be relieved to see the back of each other.

Speaking of John's back, there it was, barring the hallway to the elevators. Her heart rate rose just at the sight of him, which was ridiculous. He stood in conversation with a young payroll employee named Tricia.

"Good night," she muttered as she skirted carefully around them.

"Constance!" His voice boomed through her consciousness. "Come down and watch the action on the floor with me. It really picks up in the evenings. You should see the place when it's busy."

"No, thanks. I need to get back to the hotel." She kept her eyes focused on the far end of the hallway. But he moved past her and pressed the button for the elevator before she reached it.

"You're knocking off work to relax when you should be examining the details of our operations? I'm shocked, Constance."

Her gaze darted to him as an urge to defend herself rushed over her. "It's really just the paperwork that interests me."

He lifted a dark brow. "I think you're being remiss in your duties. I'd think the BIA would want to know all the gory details of how we operate. I wouldn't be surprised if they wanted a full report on everyone who works here."

"They'll need to hire a private investigator for that. I'm an accountant." The elevator opened and she dived in. Of course he came right after her.

His proximity did something really annoying to her body temperature. Suddenly she was sweating inside her conservative suit. Maybe her new blouse had too much synthetic fabric in it. She felt a frown form on her brow and attempted to smooth it away. She didn't want him to know that his presence rattled her so much.

"You've only observed the casino during the day so far. We're virtually empty then. You should really take a look at the place during the evenings, when most of our customers are here. It's the best way to see how we do business."

He did have a point. If she were her boss, she'd tell her to stay. Should she really let her inappropriate attraction to John Fairweather prevent her from doing her job properly? "I suppose you're right. There's no need for you to accompany me, though. I don't want to bother you."

Constance saw that familiar sparkle of mischief in his dark eyes. "On the contrary. It would be my pleasure."

When the elevator doors opened, she prepared for him to try to slide his arm through hers, or take her hand, but he simply gestured for her to go first. She walked ahead of him toward the game rooms. Was he looking at her behind? She felt her hips swing a little more than usual, and immediately tried to prevent it. She was probably letting her imagination run away with her, which she confirmed when she turned to find him texting on his phone.

He's not attracted to you, Constance. Why would he be? He just kissed you because he could. He's that kind of man.

"Let's get you a drink."

"No!" The protest flew from her mouth so loudly it made her glance around.

He smiled. "We have fresh-squeezed fruit juice at the bars. Leon does an amazing concoction of fresh pineapple juice with fresh coconut milk and a dash of his secret spices. Totally nonalcoholic."

"That does sound good." Coconut milk was supposed to be healthy and she'd never tried it.

He ordered two of the drinks, which arrived in large glass goblets with the casino's sunrise logo on them. He lifted his glass. "Here's to you discovering everything there is to know about us, and liking what you see."

She merely nodded. She wasn't supposed to hope that she'd like everything she saw. That would discourage her from looking for problems. She sipped her drink, though, and found it creamy and delicious. "I admit this is really good. I usually just drink soda when I'm out. I guess I'll have to branch out."

"I'm always asking them to invent new beverages. There's no reason why us nondrinkers should be left out in the cold."

"You don't drink alcohol?"

"Nope. I steer well clear of it. It killed my mom."

"What? I thought she was really young when she died."

"She was twenty. She died in a car wreck. Drove off an overpass. It would never have happened if she'd been sober."

"I'm so sorry."

"Me, too. I don't remember her at all. I was only six months old when she died. Luckily for me, she'd left me with a friend for the night. My grandparents made me swear never to touch the stuff and I've never seen a reason to defy them."

"Very sensible." Her prim reply embarrassed her. John had endured a devastating loss. It must be so odd to grow up not knowing the woman who gave birth to you. "Do you get mad at her for not being there for you?"

He paused, and looked right at her with a curious expression in his eyes. "Yes. When I was younger I was angry with her for not being more careful. Seems crazy, really. It does make me keep a close eye on the younger kids here, though. Especially the ones who've moved away from family to join us. I'm a big fan of stern lectures."

She smiled. "You sound like my parents. I grew up on a steady diet of stern lectures."

"And look how well you turned out."

"Some would say I'm far too conservative for my own good."

"And I'd be one of them." He winked. "Still, that's better than some of the alternatives. Let's go watch the roulette tables."

"You're not going to make me play, are you?"

He laughed. "I'm not going to make you do anything you don't want to."

What was it about Constance that got under his skin? John stood next to her as the wheel spun and the ball danced between black and red. She was so unlike the usual stream of glamorous women who hung around him, sniffing the scent of money or promising a steamy affair.

Constance stood with her arms crossed over her prim

suit, eyes fixed firmly on the table and not a hint of flirtation in her gestures.

But he knew she was as attracted to him as he was to her. The shine in her eyes when she looked at him, the glow in her cheeks, the way she angled her body toward him unconsciously—it all spoke of the desire that crackled between them so forcefully you could almost hear it snap in the air.

She didn't want to like him. Or to want him. But somehow that only heightened the tension building as they stood next to each other, pretending to focus on the white ball.

It dropped into a slot and the wheel slowed to a halt. One woman squealed with delight and smiled as the croupier slid a pile of chips toward her. John glanced at Constance and saw the tiny hint of a smile that hovered about her pretty mouth. "That's why they keep coming back," he said softly.

"I can see how it would be fun." She leaned into him so he could hear her but no one else could. Her scent tugged at his sense. "But I'd still rather make money the old-fashioned way."

"Me, too. I'll take hard work over chance any day of the week." He leaned still closer until he could almost feel the heat of her skin. "But everyone's different."

Did he like her because she was different? It didn't really make sense. There was no good reason to flirt with and tempt this woman. She was here on professional business and it was inappropriate for him to even have sensual thoughts about her.

Yet he couldn't seem to stop.

As he'd promised, he had no intention of making her do anything she didn't want to. But making her want to? That was a whole different story.

* * *

One time at a college mixer someone had given Constance a glass of orange juice mixed with vodka—without mentioning the vodka. She still remembered the way the world around her had grown blurry, and she'd found herself laughing at things that weren't even funny. She felt like that right now, though she was sure she'd had nothing but fruit juice all evening.

"...and then after we won every game that season, they wouldn't let me go." John leaned into her again, brushing her arm with his. Her skin sizzled inside her suit. "It was a pain in the ass. All I wanted to do was study statistics, and I had to get all this tiresome fresh air and sunshine."

She laughed. He'd been telling her about how he'd joined the college football team entirely for the scholarship money and then accidentally became their star player. Of course he had. He was one of those people who effortlessly succeeded at everything they tried. Or maybe not effortlessly. He just made it look that way.

"It must get annoying being so good at everything."

"You think I'm bragging?"

"I'm pretty sure of it." She narrowed her eyes, trying to hide her smile. He hadn't really volunteered any information she hadn't asked for. She wanted to know more about him. At first she told herself she was doing "research." Now she was too darn curious to stop. "What did your team members think of you?"

"Oh, at first they made fun of me. Teased me for being from the backwoods of Massachusetts. They stopped laughing when they saw how fast I could run, though."

"Can you still run fast?" Her hand accidentally brushed his as she raised her drink to her lips. They'd moved to a sofa near the blackjack tables, where they had a good view of the whole room. Her thigh jostled against his, too. The sofa was soft and they kept sinking into it. The crowds milled about the gaming tables, ignoring them completely.

"I don't know. I haven't tried lately. I'm still pretty quick on the squash court, though. Do you play any sports?"

"No." Maybe she should start. All this energy building up inside her needed some place to go. Right now she felt like jumping up and running around the room. "My parents thought sports were a waste of time."

"And you never did anything they didn't want you to?"

"Nothing major. I read some books they didn't approve of, and they never knew I had a boyfriend."

"You kept your lover a secret from them?" He bumped against her, teasing.

"It wasn't like that."

"No? It certainly sounds like it."

"He was at college with me in a different town, so they never met him."

"And you didn't mention him. Was he someone they wouldn't have approved of?" He raised a brow.

She chuckled. "No. That's the funny part. He was so dull they'd probably have liked him." Was she really talking about Phil? She'd tried to shove him out of her mind. Which was hard, because six years later he was still the only boyfriend she'd ever had.

At least now she could admit he wasn't exactly the man of her dreams.

"Why were you dating him if he was dull?"

"I like dull."

John peered into her eyes. The effect of his dark gaze was anything but dull. Sensations she'd never felt before trickled through every part of her. "Why?"

"Predictable. Reassuring. I don't enjoy surprises."

"Or at least you think you don't." One brow lifted slightly. "Come with me."

He took her hand gently and helped her up from the squishy sofa. “Where are we going?”

“It’s a surprise.”

“I already told you I don’t like them.” Anticipation rippled in her tummy.

“I don’t believe you.” He led her across the busy game room to the bank of shiny elevators. Her hand pulsed inside his. They were walking along like a couple, and while it horrified her, the realization gave her a strange thrill. She should pull her hand from his, but she didn’t.

He pressed the button for the highest floor and shot her a mysterious look.

“I’m not even going to ask,” she murmured, trying to keep her eyes on the door. Even while she knew he was flirting with her and leading her on, she trusted John not to pull any fast moves. They’d been talking for a while and he was clearly a man who took the concept of personal honor seriously. He saw himself as a role model for the younger members of the tribe and he’d said more than once that he never did anything he wouldn’t want them to know about.

Of course, maybe he was just trying to undermine her defenses by appearing principled and thoughtful.

What a shame it was working.

The elevator opened at the top floor and she was surprised when the doors parted to reveal the night sky. “Wow, a roof terrace.” A broad expanse of marble, ringed with potted plants, glowed under the stars. “How come there’s no one up here?”

“It’s not open to the public unless it’s booked for an event and, as you can see, there’s nothing happening here tonight except us.”

Us. What did he mean by that? Nothing, probably. “That’s a lot of stars.” She felt as though she could see forever, bright galaxies twinkling all the way to infinity.

"It's nice being up here above all the lights. You can see clearly. I come up here when I need to get perspective."

"Feeling like a tiny speck in the vast universe certainly puts everything in perspective."

"Doesn't it, though? All the worries that keep us little humans awake at night are nothing in the grand scheme of things."

He still held her hand, which had grown quite hot. They walked across the terrace to a seating area and he guided her onto a large sofa and sat down next to her.

What am I doing? Up here there was no pretense that they were still working. Or that she was researching anything. She was simply sitting with John, her right thigh fully pressed against his left one as they both sank into the soft cushions. The cool night air emphasized the warmth of his body.

"What do you worry about, Constance?" His hand squeezed hers very gently.

"Sometimes I worry that I'll never move out of my parents' house." She laughed, trying to lighten the moment.

"Why haven't you? You must earn enough to rent your own place."

"I don't know, really. I keep thinking that I will, then another month or year passes and I'm still there."

"Maybe you've been waiting to meet the right man."

"Probably." The confession surprised her. "After all, I've always been told a nice girl is supposed to live at home until she gets married." She shrugged.

"Why haven't you met the right person yet?"

"I work at an accounting firm. It's not exactly a hotbed of romance." She smiled.

"Don't accountants need love, too?"

"Apparently so." Was he trying to suggest that she go back and date one of her coworkers? That would be a strange suggestion from a man still holding her hand in his. "Why haven't *you* married?" Curiosity pricked at her, even though she was pretty sure she knew the answer. Why would a man in John's position want to settle down with one woman when he could have a different one every week if he wanted?

"I have been."

His answer shocked her so much she tried to pull her hand from his. "You're divorced?" Her hand flew free, and the chill night air assaulted her hot palm.

He nodded. "A long time ago. You're shocked."

"I didn't read that when I was researching you."

"It's not common knowledge. I was married in high school, right before I went away to college. I thought it would help keep us together despite the physical distance."

"Which was only a hundred miles or so."

"Less than fifty, actually." He grinned. "Young and stupid."

"Why did you split up?"

"I was so busy with school that I didn't make enough time for her and she met someone else. It proved to me that a marriage isn't something that just happens. It takes a lot of work to keep it alive."

"And that scared you off trying it again?" She attempted to pull her thigh away from his but once again the sofa was too deep and she kept falling against him.

"Pretty much." His eyes twinkled in the darkness. "I know I've got my hands full with my business, and now with running the tribe, so I don't want to disappoint some-one else."

"Oh." She felt a surprising sting of disappointment, which annoyed her. Had she really imagined somewhere in the darkest recesses of her mind that John might have real feelings for her? She was getting carried away! "So you probably won't get married again."

"I damn sure will." His conviction startled her. "Don't count me out yet."

"I can see you feel strongly about it." Her smile matched his. How did he keep doing that to her? Any sensible woman would leap to her feet and go admire the view on the far side of the patio, away from this man who freely admitted he didn't have time for a relationship.

"Oh, I do feel strongly about it. In addition to any personal considerations, I have a responsibility to the Nissequot tribe to help produce the next generation." He winked.

She couldn't help laughing. "That's a weighty responsibility. Does it mean you have to marry another Nissequot?"

"Nope." His gaze grew more serious. "We made sure there were no requirements for any particular amount of Indian blood in tribal members. I hate the idea that people have to choose who they marry carefully or abandon their heritage."

"I'd imagine those kinds of rules are in place to keep the benefits—government funds, casino profits and that kind of thing—to a limited number of people."

"And what good does that do anyone? Except the people trying to keep us small in the hope that we'll fade away eventually. I'd prefer to expand to include everyone. Growth and change are the core facts of life. If you try to keep something static, it will just die. I'm here to make sure the opposite happens." He took her hand again, and she didn't pull it back. He lifted it to his lips and kissed her palm, which sizzled with awareness under his lips.

Why did she let him do that? He wasn't serious about her. He was playing with her.

Or was he?

His dark eyes had narrowed and fixed on hers with an

expression so intense that she couldn't breathe. Heat radiated through her and her body inched closer to his without any effort on her part. She should be trying to back away, or standing up and walking back to the elevator. But her entire body seemed to be in thrall to his.

His lips touched hers very softly, just brushing them. It wasn't even a kiss. She closed her eyes as she drank in the subtle male scent of him. Her tongue itched to meet his, which it did as their mouths opened slightly and welcomed each other into a real kiss.

Her fingers crept under the jacket of his suit and into the folds of his shirt. His large hands settled one on either side of her waist, gathering her to him. She was aware of the roughness of his chin as he shifted and deepened the kiss. She leaned into him, pulling at his shirt until her fingers slid underneath it and she touched the warm skin of his back.

Heat unfurled in her core, spreading through her like smoke. John lifted her onto his lap, still kissing her, and she welcomed the closeness. Her nipples were so sensitive she could feel the fabric of his lapels even through her blouse and bra, and she pressed herself against him, unable to resist the pull of sensation.

She had no idea how long they kissed. All she knew was that she didn't want to stop. The pleasure of holding him, of touching him and kissing him, was so intense she couldn't remember anything like it. When their lips finally separated slightly, she could barely pull herself together enough to open her eyes.

"There's something very powerful between us," John murmured, his voice a rumble in her consciousness.

"Yes," she whispered. Words seemed too literal in the heady sensual atmosphere of the dark night. It was easier to say what she wanted with her body, with her mouth. She licked his lips gently, savoring the taste of him. When his hand moved higher, she guided it over her breast, enjoying the weight of his palm on her desire-thickened nipple.

When he pulled back she uttered a groan of protest. She didn't want him to stop.

"Come with me." He lifted her carefully to her feet, supporting her with his arm. She was so intoxicated with arousal that she could barely walk.

"Where are we going?" It was hard forming words.

"Somewhere more private."

"This is private." No one was watching them. Only the twinkling gaze of a hundred million stars. She didn't want to leave. She didn't want anything to break the spell binding them together.

"More comfortable, too." He squeezed her. "Don't worry. It's close." They walked slowly back to the elevator, with his arm around her waist. The effort of putting one foot in front of the other tugged her out of the sensual haze she'd slipped into. What was she doing? She'd kissed John again. Kissing him one time could be seen as an accident. Kissing him twice? That was deliberate.

She wanted to kiss him again, too. What had come over her? She must be in the grip of some kind of madness. Still, she wasn't going to pull away from the warm embrace of his arm. Instead she rested her hand on his, enjoying the closeness.

At the elevator he pressed the button. "Are we going down to the lobby?"

He looked rather disheveled from her running her hands all over him. She probably did, too. "No need to. The elevator also leads directly into my suite."

"Oh, good." Her own words made her blink. She was glad about him taking her to his private apartment?

Yes. She was. Which didn't make any sense at all. She

should insist on going straight to her car and back to her hotel for a cold shower.

They stepped into the unpleasantly bright space of the elevator and she shielded her eyes from the shining mirrors by leaning against his chest as he pressed the button. His suite was on the highest floor, right beneath the roof terrace, so in a few seconds the doors opened and they stepped out, right into his suite.

"Do strangers from the hotel ever press the wrong button and end up in your room?"

He smiled and shook his head. "You have to enter a code to go to this floor or the terrace. Don't worry. No one will disturb us."

They stepped out into his suite. A wide foyer led into a spacious living room with a wall of windows. Comfortable sofas faced what must have been an impressive view in daylight. Shelves held a collection of photographs and objects. She was curious about the things he had gathered in his home, but he led her past them and through another door into his bedroom. Decorated in a simple, masculine style, the room held nothing but a low platform bed and a dresser. Three wooden masks hung on the wall opposite. She stared at them for a moment. "Don't you feel weird with these faces watching you?"

He laughed. "They're hundreds of years old. I'm sure they've seen it all before."

No doubt they'd seen a lot right here in John's bedroom. She glanced warily at the bed. How many women had writhed in his arms there? Was she really going to be the next in a long procession of girls who succumbed to his seemingly irresistible charms? What was she doing? She knew she shouldn't be here, but she didn't want to be anywhere else.

John turned to her, slid his arms around her waist and

held her close. He was several inches taller, so he had to incline his head to kiss her. Her mouth rose effortlessly to meet his and the kiss drew her back into that private realm where nothing else really mattered.

Six

John sensed her doubts even as he kissed her. Constance could hardly believe she was here in his bedroom. He could hardly believe it either. Still, his disbelief mingled with a sense of wonder as he held her close and kissed her with feeling.

She didn't have much experience. He could tell that by her sense of surprise and her awkward reaction to his simple advances. Somehow that only stoked his passion. This beautiful woman had been quietly living her life, free from desire and its complications, peering into corporate records and keeping her heart safe.

Constance was like a safe with a long and complicated combination, and his fingers itched to turn the dial until she clicked open for him. The image appealed to him. He wanted to unlock the door to her heart and let himself in.

He helped her carefully out of her suit jacket and laid it on the chair. Her blouse had a silky texture and he could feel the warmth of her body through it, so he let himself enjoy the sensation of her skin through the fabric while he kissed her.

Then he started to unbutton it. First just one button. Then another kiss. Then the second button. More kissing. Her eyes opened slightly as he went for the third button, and the sparkle of excitement in them fired his arousal.

Her hands roamed under his shirt, feeling the muscle along his back. When they dipped into the waistband of his pants, the sudden rush of sensation made him gasp. He was so hard it was difficult to be patient and careful with her, but that was the only way to unlock her closely guarded safe and enjoy the intimacy he craved. He knew he'd blow everything if he tried to rush. He wanted this to be as enjoyable for her as he knew it would be for him.

He guided her to the edge of the bed and sat her gently down, then knelt in front of her and pulled her shirt back to reveal her bra. She watched him curiously, eyes shining, as he lowered his mouth over her breast and dampened the fabric of her bra with his tongue. Already firm, her nipple thickened under his caress, and she let out a small murmur of pleasure.

She ran her fingers through his hair, encouraging him as he licked and sucked first one breast and then the other. Then he lowered his head to trace a line down toward her belly button. She inhaled sharply as he reached the waistband of her skirt.

"Lie back," he murmured, stroking her cheek with his thumb.

She blinked, not questioning anything, then eased herself down onto the soft bedcover. Her thighs clenched together as he unbuttoned the top of her skirt—which opened at the side—and started to slide it down her shapely legs.

He wanted to tell her to relax, but had a feeling that words might have the opposite effect. Sometimes it was better to touch than talk.

The removal of her skirt revealed pretty lace-trimmed panties that rather surprised him. He'd expected utilitarian cotton. And she must have bought them since the fire. Had she known he'd see and enjoy them? Had she bought them for him? It was hard to imagine, but the thought made him smile.

He didn't part her legs, which she still pressed together tightly, although he longed to taste her through the lacy fabric. Instead he kissed her thighs, her knees and her legs right down to her toes. She softened and relaxed as he traveled along her smooth skin.

He ventured tentatively toward her female center, wanting to explore every delicious inch of her. The soft silk of her panties didn't conceal the heat radiating from her core. She flinched slightly as he flicked his tongue over her, then whimpered softly as he sucked her through the delicate fabric.

Once she was thoroughly relaxed and pulsing with heat and pleasure, all resistance kneaded away, he slid off her shirt. She eagerly reached for his shirt buttons, tugging at them, as a smile spread across her face. Her hungry energy surprised him. She wanted to see him naked almost as much as he wanted to be naked with her. Together they undid his belt and shed his pants, and pulled off his shirt. Then she hesitated, frowning slightly, staring at his briefs.

He was aroused almost to the point of madness, and it showed. He wondered for a second if she'd freeze up and try to backtrack—something that just might kill him at this moment. Instead he almost died anyway when she slid her fingers inside the waistband of his underwear and took hold of him.

Constance couldn't remember being this aroused *ever.* Part of her couldn't believe she had her fingers wrapped gently but firmly around John's impressive erection. The rest of her really wanted to feel him inside her right now.

She heard his sharp intake of breath as she stroked him. It gave her a thrill that he was so excited, too.

"Hold on," he rasped. "Before we get carried away and forget."

He reached into a nearby dresser and brought out a condom packet. She hadn't even thought about contraception. She wasn't on the pill, either. Why would she be? Obviously common sense had deserted her.

Sheathed, he came close and she wrapped her hand around him again. Her body was almost trembling with anticipation as she guided him into her, not that he needed any help, and he lowered his chest over hers. He kissed her very softly right as he entered her—so slow and careful—and she felt her hips lift to greet his.

The powerful sensation of him inside her quickened her breath. She could feel her fingers clawing at his back, traveling into his hair, but she didn't seem to have any control over them. Luckily that didn't matter because he took control, moving with gentle intensity, driving her further and further into an intense world of pleasure and passion.

"I'm crazy about you," he whispered in her ear, as her breath quickened to the point of gasping. The sensation of his hot breath on her ear only heightened her pleasure.

"Me, too." Did that even make any sense? Nothing made sense, except kissing him more and reveling in the sensation of him deep inside her. His big body moved over hers with ease, shifting position to send her closer yet to the brink of...something.

Sensation was building inside her and she became more aware of it as John sucked her earlobe gently while filling her over and over again. Something was creeping through her, a wave of pleasure, or a whole tide of it, starting in the clenched tips of her toes and rising up her legs and sweeping over her belly until she felt as though she was drowning in it. Distant moaning and shrieking sounds might have come from her mouth, but she couldn't be sure. John uttered a low groan and gathered her so tightly in his arms she thought she might disappear into him completely. She wanted to say something but she couldn't make a sound, just little gasps that burst from her lips onto the hot skin of his shoulder as he clung to her.

"Am I crushing you?" John eased himself off her slightly by propping himself on his elbows.

"No." His powerful physique felt no heavier than a down comforter, enveloping her in its warmth. "You feel fantastic."

"You, too." He kissed her so softly she almost wanted to cry.

Cry? Strange emotions suddenly welled up inside her. She didn't even really know what had happened. Was that an orgasm? She'd read about them but had never come close to experiencing one before. Her body still pulsed and tingled with the aftereffects. Her heart squeezed and she held John close. She felt incredibly intimate with him right now. Which wasn't surprising, considering that they were both naked in his bed.

On his bed. With the lights on.

Her eyes cracked open as she managed to regain some grip on her consciousness. They hadn't even taken the time to climb under the covers. In fact, they weren't even at the right end of the bed.

She swallowed, trying to make sense of what had just happened. John stroked a tendril of damp hair from her forehead. "You're very passionate, Constance."

Coming from his mouth, her dull and prim name seemed sensual and evocative. "So are you, John." His name was even duller than hers, and he was the most exciting and intriguing man she'd ever met. Apparently names didn't have too much to do with anything.

"Let's get under the covers." A smile shone in his eyes.

"Okay." She let him lift her, her body feeling almost weightless in his strong embrace, and slide her under the soft white covers. Then he settled next to her and wrapped his arms around her. A soft kiss on her cheek felt so romantic she thought for a second that she must be dreaming.

She wasn't, though. There was no way she could conjure the intoxicating scent of his skin in a dream. Or the slightly rough feel of his cheek against hers, or the sparkle of amusement—and passion—in his eyes. This was real, and it was happening to her, Constance Allen, right here, right now.

"I really don't know how I ended up here." She felt like being honest.

"It's the most natural thing in the world. Two people being attracted to each other and wanting to be together."

"I don't get why you're attracted to me, though." No doubt any dating manual would issue stern warnings against such a blatant display of insecurity. But she couldn't help wondering what John Fairweather saw in her.

He wanted her, there was no doubt about that. She could feel it in the way he looked at her, in the way he made love to her, in the way he held her close, his breath on her cheek.

"I don't know where you've gotten the idea that you're not desirable. You're a beautiful woman." He stroked her cheek with his thumb.

"I am not! I'm quite ordinary looking."

"Who told you that? You have the prettiest hazel eyes I've ever seen. So curious and a little wary. When you look at me I get a jolt of something I can't explain."

Her eyes? "But I wear glasses. Where are they, anyway?"

"On the chest over there. I made sure to put them somewhere safe."

"I don't even remember taking them off." She reached

automatically for her nose, where she usually pushed them up.

"You didn't. I did." His smile made her smile—as usual. "Apparently you can see pretty well without them."

"I just need them for reading. They're a mild prescription." She could see John clearly enough right now, his dark eyes peering into hers.

"So how come you wear them all the time?"

She shrugged, or attempted to, in his arms. "I feel more comfortable with them on. Then I don't have to worry about taking them on and off to read. I do spend a lot of time reading, even if it's mostly numbers."

"Something to hide behind. I don't think you're comfortable with your own beauty."

She laughed. "I don't think I'm comfortable with much of anything, except doing my job to the best of my ability. And right now I'm not doing so well with that, either."

"Because you're sleeping with the subject of your investigation?"

"Who's sleeping?"

He chuckled. "Do you feel guilty?"

"Of course. Don't you?"

"For seducing you? No, I don't feel at all guilty. Like I said, it's the most natural thing in the world for two people who are drawn to each other to enjoy each other's company."

Of course it was, to him. That's why he had so many girlfriends. He probably never said no when he saw something, or someone, he wanted. "My boss would kill me if she knew I was in bed with you right now."

"She won't find out." He lowered his lips to hers in a soft kiss.

No. She wouldn't. This little…affair—because there

was no better word for it—had to be kept under wraps. Which meant it was wrong.

If Constance had any sense she'd push John off her right now and run screaming back to her hotel.

But she didn't want to. She wanted to lie here in his arms, to feel his rough cheek against hers. To enjoy the warm, protective embrace of his strong arms and his satisfied sigh in her ear. In fact she couldn't remember the last time she felt so completely relaxed and content.

She'd spent too many lonely nights in her bedroom. Too many solitary hours dreaming of moments like this. Everyone, including her own parents, thought she had no feelings at all. That she lived to work. That her brain was filled with numbers and spreadsheets and she spent all her spare time doing elaborate computations. But she was just like everyone else, though she hid it well. She craved companionship, romance, love.

Love? Well, she wasn't going to find that with John Fairweather. A tiny stab of regret poked at her heart. She could probably fall in love with him quite easily on the briefest acquaintance. Despite his reputation as a callous, money-orientated playboy, she'd learned he was a man of principle who put those principles into practice every day. The media was so wrong about him. Or maybe they were jealous. She could now grow quite angry thinking about the callous things she'd read about him and the tribe.

"Your heart's beating faster." His gruff voice tickled something deep inside her.

"I was just thinking about how wrong everyone is about you."

He laughed. "Are they, though? I don't lose a single moment of sleep worrying what other people think. I don't care about them at all. Maybe that's what they hate the most."

"I admire your independent spirit."

"Do you?" He sounded surprised. "I thought you were convinced that everything I stand for is wrong."

"That's when I thought you stood for gambling and drinking and cheating people out of their hard-earned money. Now I know those things are means to an end. You wouldn't be in the gambling business at all if it weren't for you trying to build the tribe, would you?"

He watched her for a moment. "I admit, the software business was a lot less complicated." A smile tugged at his mouth. "In fact, I'm planning to get back into it. We've been working on some database software to improve our business operations here and I plan to release a beta version in the next three months or so."

"Maybe it will be more successful than the casino."

"That's hard to imagine, but you never know."

"Most people would be resting on their laurels and enjoying the fruits of their hard work, but you're always trying something new."

"Maybe I'm just restless." He shifted, bumping against her and stirring desire.

"I'm not like that at all." She let out a sigh. "I'm very dull, really. I don't have any desire to set the world on fire. I'm just trying to save enough to buy my own house and move out."

"The world would be a crazy place if everyone was like me. Can you imagine? A blend of different types of people is much more peaceful and productive." He kissed her cheek.

Her skin stirred under his lips. "I suppose you're right." Was that why he liked her—she provided a pleasantly dull contrast to his high-octane self?

"Opposites attract." He squeezed her, and she reveled in the sensation of his big body pressed against hers.

"Apparently so." She caressed the thick muscle of his back. It was hard to believe she lay here in his arms, completely naked. It felt oddly natural. As had their lovemaking. Much more so than the hurried fumblings with the college boyfriend she'd planned to spend the rest of her life with.

Right now she could easily imagine herself and John having an actual relationship. Surely they were already, to a certain extent? Except that she was here to investigate his company for improprieties and she'd probably be fired if anyone found out about this.

"What's the matter?" He must have heard her breathing quicken.

"I can't believe we're in bed together."

He paused, and stroked her shoulder. "Nothing happens by accident."

"No? I didn't plan this and I don't think you did, either."

His chest rumbled with a chuckle. "You're right. But we can both be discreet."

She wasn't sure if it was a question or a command. Either way it hurt. Which it shouldn't have, because she certainly didn't want him telling anyone. "Of course."

No promises. No expectations.

No future.

She'd fallen into his arms knowing this was crazy, but she hadn't been able to help herself. Too many nights in her lonely bedroom, wondering if a man would ever hold her again. Too many dreams that hadn't come true. The last few years of loneliness had apparently left her in a desperate and dangerous condition and brought her here into John Fairweather's bed.

"We're not entirely opposites, you know." John kissed her cheek softly.

"No? How are we similar?"

"We're both stubborn and determined."

"I think I'm going to take that as an insult. I was raised to be obedient and compliant." She raised a brow.

"Well, something went wrong." He winked, and the sparkle of humor in his eyes did something strange to her belly. "Because I can tell you make up your own mind about everything."

"What makes you say that?"

"You're here, aren't you? In my arms." He squeezed her gently, and her heart tripped a little.

"I'm not sure my mind was involved in this at all. I suspect other, less intellectual parts of my body were involved."

His chest rocked with laughter. "To a certain extent, yes, but you're here and thinking right now and I don't notice you running for the door."

"Trust me, I'm thinking about running for the door." She glanced at it, as if to make sure the way was clear.

"Guess I'll have to keep a tight hold on you, then." His arms circled her completely, which felt fabulous. She didn't want to move from their embrace. "Because I don't want you to go."

"I'm sure you'd have no trouble finding someone to take my place here." She regretted the jealous-sounding words the moment they came out.

"I'm not at all interested in anyone else. I bet you'd be surprised by how long it's been since I slept with a woman."

"Really?" Her own curiosity embarrassed her.

"I won't lie. I sowed some wild oats when I was younger, especially after my marriage fell apart. I'd been a true romantic up until then and I couldn't believe that the forever she'd promised me had turned out to be less than a year. I probably got revenge on myself more than anyone else. I was mad at myself for trusting her."

"I was mad at myself for trusting in my ex. And he didn't even cheat on me. At least not that I know of."

"It's hard to put your faith in other people once you've been let down. Is that why you haven't been serious with anyone else?"

She paused, not wanting to tell the truth. But she wasn't really cut out for fibbing. "No one's even asked me out since then."

"In five or six years?" His incredulity made her bite her lip.

"Nope. Not once." Maybe that explained why she'd leaped so willingly into John's entirely unsuitable arms.

"That's insane. You are kind of intimidating, though. It probably takes someone as obnoxious as me to be arrogant enough to try."

"Intimidating? I think of myself as being humble and unassuming."

His deep belly laugh rocked her. "You can think of yourself that way all you want. The truth is you're a demanding and rather judgmental woman who probably scares the pants off most men."

"Oh." She frowned. "That doesn't sound good."

"I like it." His grin warmed her. "If you have high expectations of yourself, you should have them of others, too. I know I do."

"Hmm. Now that you put it like that, it doesn't seem so bad." Her head rested on his bicep, which was more comfortable than the softest pillow. "I suppose you're right that a lot of people find me unapproachable. I turn down so many lunch invitations and weekend plans from coworkers that people rarely invite me anywhere anymore."

"Why do you turn them down?"

"I think they're silly. I go to the office to work, not socialize."

"See? You are unapproachable." His grin revealed those even white teeth. "They're right to be afraid. What about your church? You said your family is religious. Didn't you meet anyone there?"

"Not anyone I was interested in."

"So you're also picky." He stroked a tendril of hair off her cheek.

"Shouldn't I be? What's the point of pretending you like someone when you don't?"

"None whatsoever." He grinned. "I guess that means you like me."

"I wouldn't say that," she teased. Why was he so easy to talk to? "But apparently I am attracted to you."

"And I'm attracted to you." His gentle kiss made her lips tingle. "There's some serious chemistry between us."

There was. It snapped in the air and sensitized her skin where their bodies touched. Pheromones. Mysterious substances that science barely understood, which coaxed humans into situations any sane person would avoid. Like lying cheek to cheek with the man whose business you were investigating.

"It's a shame chemistry doesn't last and that after a while you have to actually be compatible and get along." She wanted to let him know she didn't expect this crazy fling to go anywhere. Or maybe she just wanted to reject him before he could reject her.

"You have to start somewhere." He kissed her again. She wished he'd stop doing that! It stirred all kinds of sensations deep in her belly. Sensations that made her wish he were inside her again. What kind of woman had he turned her into? "How do you know we're not perfectly compatible?"

"Us? That's funny." She didn't want him to think his words had any effect on her, but they did. They were both good with numbers. Both hardworking and determined. She would have once said that he was a notorious playboy and she was the exact opposite, but her current position here in his arms proved that she wasn't so entirely different from him when the opportunity for romance presented itself.

Romance? Where had that word come from? There wasn't anything terribly romantic about their relationship so far. Romance was flirtation and candlelit dinners and hopeful conversations. They'd gone straight from zero to sixty with very little preamble.

She'd better not let herself start thinking that this was a romance, or she was likely to end up with a broken heart.

"I don't think it's so funny at all. My grandparents are very different and they've been together for almost fifty years. He was wild and considered himself a beatnik. He wrote terrible poetry and played the trumpet, and he was getting ready to run away to New York and become a jazz musician when he met my grandmother while delivering milk to a local depot. She'd just moved here with her family from Minnesota and had never dated or kissed a boy in her life. She was training to become a schoolteacher and spent her evenings reading and knitting. He charmed her and she tamed him and they've been together ever since."

"Oh." A dangerous charmer and a good girl. Sounded familiar.

"He was very good-looking. She always said that she never stood a chance against him."

"Have they been happy?" She was genuinely curious. People always talked about those opposites-attract relationships, but she didn't know how often they really worked out.

"Very. They've had their ups and downs, of course. My mom—the one who gave birth to me—was even wilder than my grandfather when he was young, and it ended up killing her. Her death put a strain on their relationship, as a child's death often does. My grandmother blamed my grandfather for not being stricter with her, and he blamed her for not being more accepting. He felt that if my mom had still lived at home maybe she wouldn't have gone out drinking and driving on the night she died."

"If things were different, maybe you wouldn't have been born." She stroked the wrinkle that had formed between his brows. "So much of life depends on chance."

She'd never had that thought before. She was a planner, and unapologetic about it. She'd had her whole life mapped out from about age eleven: she'd intended to meet and marry a nice, appropriate spouse during college, then work for several years to build their finances and buy a house before they started a family. She'd planned her career in accounting and made sure to keep abreast of all developments in the field so she'd always have in-demand skills. When her marriage plans had derailed, she'd continued full speed ahead with the other elements of her life blueprint, assuming that everything would slot into place eventually, even if not on her anticipated schedule. She hadn't spent a single moment thinking about the rather scary mechanics of chance.

"You're right. All the hard work in the world won't get you anywhere without at least a dash of luck, too. I can't tell you how many times the fate of this casino, even the whole tribe, rested on a decision made by strangers who didn't have any real stake in the outcome. There were certainly enough people hoping that it wouldn't happen. And plenty that would like to shut us down right now."

"Do you think that's what they would do if I found

that you were actually cooking your books?" Her stomach clenched. She could probably wreak havoc on John's entire existence.

"I don't doubt that they'd try. Believe me, it makes it easy to stay honest."

"Why are so many people opposed to the casino?"

"Well, there are the people who are against it for the same reasons as you." He touched her lips with a finger. "You know, gambling, drinking, people wasting time having fun. But I suspect even more of them are just jealous. They think we're getting away with something. Enjoying some benefit that they can't have because they're not Indian. No one likes to feel excluded."

"I suppose you're right, but isn't it supposed to be a reparation of sorts for past injustices?"

"I think some people see it that way, especially people who are trying to justify their gambling losses as a charitable donation." He winked. "But really it's just a recognition of past treaties, allowing us sovereignty over our own lands and people. So many of these agreements were ignored or broken over the centuries, and now things are changing. There's no element of payback in it. If anything you'd think Americans would be glad that we're finally getting with the program and embracing the complicated laws and unbridled capitalism that have made this country so powerful and influential."

John was so charming it was hard to imagine anyone disagreeing with him once they'd talked to him face-to-face. "So basically, you're just trying to fit in."

"Exactly." His wicked grin made her smile in response. And kiss him. She couldn't help herself. Something about him had totally undermined her defenses. He kissed her back. It was warm and invigorating, and soon he had to reach for another condom.

Bliss filled her as John entered her again, banishing the years of loneliness and wanting. Her body blossomed under his affectionate caresses, and her inhibitions faded away as their intimacy deepened. Was it really this easy to find happiness with another person?

She drifted off to sleep in his calm embrace, feeling utterly at peace with the world. Right now she could easily imagine herself and John as a couple, sharing their days and nights, their thoughts, their dreams.

Could this taste of paradise turn into her real life?

Seven

Constance awoke with a jolt. Sunlight streamed through a crack in the curtains, announcing that the day was well under way.

John was gone, his side of the bed rumpled and empty.

She blinked, trying to read her watch. Ten-fifteen? She'd slept half the morning away. Why hadn't John woken her? She clutched the covers around her, trying to cover her nakedness, even though she seemed to be alone in here. Where were her clothes? She barely remembered taking them off. They were probably on the floor somewhere.

She spotted them neatly draped over a chair on the far side of the room. John must have picked them up this morning. How embarrassing! She lay here sleeping while he was up and about. Right now he was probably in a meeting or doing his daily perusal of the previous night's takings, and she was just waking up from a sensual dream.

She sprang out of bed and hurried across the room, then tried to tug her clothes on so fast it was more difficult than if she'd taken her time. She kept glancing about the room as if someone was watching. She checked her phone and saw several messages, mostly from work. There was no way she could even listen to them, never mind return the calls, while standing in John Fairweather's bedroom!

Her suit was wrinkled, probably from lying in a heap

all night. She couldn't manage to get her hair to cooperate either. She certainly hoped she could get out of here without running into anyone. And she had to drive all the way to her hotel and back before she could even get to work.

She tried to use the elevator that opened right into the suite, but she couldn't get the door to open. It required some kind of code she didn't know. Cringing with embarrassment, she cracked open the door that led into a hotel hallway. A cleaner's cart sat two doors down. She'd better get out of here before they wandered in with the vacuum. Glancing around and scurrying like a cartoon character, she darted for the public elevators at the far end of the hall.

Constance pressed the button and gritted her teeth with impatience. She couldn't remember a single occasion in her life before now that she'd needed to skulk about and conceal her shockingly inappropriate activities.

Naturally the elevator opened right into the elegant main lobby, which was unusually well populated for a weekday morning. Worse yet, she could see John giving a television interview in front of the decorative mural on the far side of the room. The cameraman with his bulky mike and the aggressively tanned male reporter almost blocked her way to the main exit, and she hesitated for a minute to plan her escape.

John hadn't seen her yet and she wanted to make sure he didn't. She didn't want him to smile and wave or otherwise draw attention to her.

"...investigated by the Bureau of Indian Affairs on suspicion of fraud..." The reporter's words assaulted her ears as she got closer. Little did they know the BIA's official investigator was trying to sneak past them wearing yesterday's underwear, with John Fairweather's DNA licked into its fabric.

John was talking now, looking directly at the reporter.

She seized her chance to break for the door, avoiding his gaze as she strode across the lobby, heels clicking. Luckily the camera was facing the other way so she wouldn't be caught on tape making her escape.

She burst out into blinding sunlight with her adrenaline pounding and fumbled for her car keys, desperate to escape before anyone saw her or tried to talk to her.

Back in her hotel room, after showering and washing away John's passionate touch, Constance called the office. "Nicola Moore of the BIA called about six times for you," Lynn whispered into the phone. "She's getting hysterical. Where have you been? There's been some kind of exposé article published about the New Dawn casino and she wants to know if it's true."

That would explain the TV reporter in the lobby. "What does it say?"

"The usual stuff, how they've grown too big too fast and it can't be legit."

"That's hardly a news story."

"There's some stuff about his uncle. I forget the guy's name but apparently he has a colorful past. Money laundering or something similar."

Constance frowned. John's uncle Don? She didn't like the guy much. He gave off a sleazebag vibe. "Everything's still checking out fine. They're very profitable because there are people here throwing their money away twenty-four hours a day."

"Are you sure you're not blinded to iniquity by John Fairweather's dazzling smile?"

"Of course I'm sure," she retorted. "Sorry. Didn't mean to sound so snappy." What a shame she couldn't explain why she hadn't gotten too much sleep last night. "I'm starting to get annoyed with all the negative opinions that keep cropping up, when I can't find any justification for them. I can't help but think people are just jealous and resent the tribe's success. Why shouldn't they have some prosperity for a change? They've been kicked around since the 1600s. It's about time they got to enjoy life a bit. I don't know why people get so upset that they're making money."

"Maybe because they don't pay taxes on it?"

"Actually, they do pay some taxes. It was built into their agreements with the state. And they provide employment in an otherwise depressed area. I've totally revised my opinion of the place and I wish everyone else would do the same."

"You sound very passionate."

Passionate? What an odd choice of word. She'd certainly experienced passion last night. It dwarfed her most ambitious daydreams. "Nonsense. I'm entirely practical. I can't see why it's okay for corporations to make money hand over fist and interpret laws to meet their needs, but not tribes. This is America. We love money and profits. You and I wouldn't have a job without them!"

Lynn laughed. "So true. Anyway, you'd better call Ms. Moore. She's getting on my nerves."

"Will do. Hopefully I'll be home in a day or two." A twinge of sadness shot through her. Once she left she probably wouldn't ever see John again. Which would make last night's tryst a one-night stand. Shame swept over her in a hot tide. She'd fallen so easily into his arms. Worse yet, she craved the feel of his arms around her right now. Of his hot kisses claiming her mouth, the powerful sensation of him moving inside her.

"Are you still there?" Lynn asked.

"Yes. Yes. Just going over some notes." Now she was lying. What next? If anyone found out that she'd had an affair with the man whose business she was supposed to be investigating, she'd be fired. She'd probably lose her accreditation and would never be able to find another job in the field.

"They must be pretty interesting notes. And you're missing some exciting happenings here at Creighton Waterman. Someone walked in on Lacey, the new trainee, getting up close and personal with Aaron Whitlow."

"What?" Mr. Whitlow was the straitlaced senior executive who gave them their annual reviews. "He must be twice her age. Maybe even three times!"

"I know. Everyone is freaking out. Worse yet, the person who saw them was Leah, the head of personnel."

"Did Lacey get fired?"

"She did. It makes me mad. Why does she have to leave? Why not him?"

"He's in a position of power."

"That's hardly fair. She should file a sexual harassment lawsuit. But she didn't want to. She said it was consensual. She was so upset, crying and red faced. I think she really cared about him."

Constance swallowed. "It is odd that relationships at work are so taboo. That is where most of us spend our time, after all."

"It's because we're supposed to behave like robots who only care about doing our jobs. Not actual people with feelings. Whitlow's acting more robotic than ever, of course. Muttering orders under his breath, looking down his snooty nose at people. It does make me laugh to picture him fooling around with a much younger woman. Apparently she was sitting on his desk with her skirt up around her waist!"

"Yikes." Constance wanted to cringe. Desire. The same thing that had lured her irresistibly into John's encouraging arms. When examined in the cold light of day, it was embarrassing and inappropriate. What would Lynn—or anyone—say if they could have seen her last night, writhing with pleasure in John's bed?

"The scandal has certainly livened things up around here, let me tell you. You're missing all the fun."

"You know I hate gossip." She tried to stay out of the petty squabbles around the watercooler.

"I'll certainly never see Whitlow in the same light again, that's for sure."

"Isn't he a widower? Maybe he was lonely." Great. Now she was defending a man who'd fooled around with a much younger employee. Of course as a transgressor herself, she could sympathize with him in a way she'd never have been able to imagine even a week ago.

Maybe this whole experience was part of her journey toward greater compassion and understanding. It was pretty humbling, all right. "I have another call coming in."

"All right. Call Nicola Moore at the BIA before she comes down there looking for you."

"Will do." She hung up and grabbed the other call, adrenaline firing because she could see it was John.

"Good morning, gorgeous."

Heat rose up from her chest. "Good morning yourself. I can't believe you let me sleep in like that. I'm so embarrassed."

"You looked so peaceful that I didn't want to disturb you. I had to get up for a media interview."

"I saw you doing it." She didn't want to say what she'd heard about the accusations against his uncle. It didn't seem appropriate given their professional relationship. Still, she wanted to hear how he'd describe it. "What were they asking you about?"

He paused for a moment. "Nothing very interesting. The usual stuff."

So he was going to hide it from her. Surely he'd know she could see it on the news or read it on the internet? "I suppose they're often hoping to stir up a story. Speaking of which, there's a sex scandal going on at my office right now. If they had any idea what I was up to I'd be out on my ear."

"I won't tell them. It's none of their business."

"I suppose not. You're not sleeping with me to cloud my judgment, are you?" She said it in jest, but once the words were out she realized she wasn't entirely kidding.

He laughed. "If I was, would it be working?"

"Of course not. I have tremendous integrity." She was trying to convince herself as much as him.

"Tremendous, huh? That is impressive. And I'd expect nothing less of you. Seriously, though, you should probably know that the media has got a wild hair about my uncle Don. I'm sure it will blow over soon, but they're trying to find him guilty of something, so you may as well hear it from me and not from the BIA."

"What do they think he's done?"

"I don't know. I don't think they care. Anything they can cook up will do. Want to get together for lunch? It's almost noon."

"Noon?" She gulped. "I can't. I'm not even at the casino. I'm still at my hotel getting changed. I need to focus completely on work for the rest of the day."

"And the night?"

"And the night." She blinked. No sense giving him a chance to make plans that were going to rope her even deeper into this impossible affair. One night with him had been intoxicating enough. Another and she might never regain her sanity. "I really need to concentrate on my work. Last night was…"

"Wonderful."

"Yes, it was." She had to admit it. "But I'm here to do a job." *And we both know this is going nowhere.*

"That's true, but I want to make sure you don't work too fast. I don't want to lose you any sooner than I have to."

So he could easily admit that their affair had a built-in end. The little pang of sorrow surprised her. "I do have other projects I need to get back to."

"It's a shame your office isn't local. Why would they hire someone from Ohio to investigate a casino in Massachusetts?"

"I think they do that to encourage impartiality. Since I'm not local, I have no stake in building or maintaining a relationship with the New Dawn casino."

"Just with its owner." His voice was silky and seductive.

"That was an accident."

"A very happy one."

"As long as no one finds out about it." And really, how happy could it be when she'd be home alone in a few days, lonely as ever?

"Concealment does not come naturally to me." She heard frustration in his voice. "In fact, I'm hating this need for secrecy. I much prefer to be frank and up front in my dealings with everyone."

"But you do understand that my job and my reputation depend on keeping this secret?" Panic gripped her quietly.

"Believe me. I do. And I hold myself entirely responsible for the delicate predicament we find ourselves in." He paused, and the silence hummed for a moment. "Can I come over to your hotel?"

She sucked in a breath as visions of John's large form in her tiny hotel room crowded her imagination. "No. I really have to work."

"Bummer." He sounded so disappointed that she had to smile.

"I have more calls to return. I'll see you at the office."

"I'll make sure of it." She could hear the smile in his voice, and it made her chest ache a little. She was really going to miss John. Which was ridiculous. She'd only known him a few days and in many ways he was the most infuriating man she'd ever met.

Yet she still liked him so much. And she liked that he'd told her about the suspicions regarding his uncle. As she dialed the number for Nicola Moore at the BIA, she was pretty sure she'd be hearing Don's name again.

She was right. Nicola immediately launched into a tirade against him.

"Don Fairweather has been previously investigated for money laundering."

"Was he convicted?" Constance glanced around her room to see if there was anything else she needed to bring to the office. It crossed her mind that she could bring a change of underwear. She told her mind to get back to business.

"No. It went to trial but the jury apparently didn't find the prosecutor's evidence convincing enough."

"Oh. So he was found innocent."

"Or they just didn't look hard enough. I want you to make sure to look in places where no one would expect. There was a case recently at another casino where three of the workers managed to pocket hundreds of thousands of dollars by creating fraudulent receipts from the slot machines to bring to the cashiers. One of them created the receipts, one was the runner between the slot machines and the tills, and the other was the cashier. As you can imagine, it was a neat little racket for a while."

"How did the casino figure out what was going on?"

"Keen observation."

"You do realize that I'm a forensic accountant and not

a private detective?" She had been told she was doing a routine audit of their books. Now that she was here, it appeared that her contact had definite suspicions, or at least was trying to plant some in her mind. That didn't sit too well with Constance when she needed to stay objective.

"Indeed, Ms. Allen, we're well aware of that. We simply expect you to find whether the paperwork is truly reflective of the casino's activities."

"I understand. I'll look into every avenue I can think of."

She hung up and found herself glancing at her underwear drawer again. What if she packed a bag with extra panties and a whole new outfit so she didn't have to come back to the hotel at all?

The blunt thought shocked her. What would her parents think if they knew what she was doing? They'd issued stern warnings about stepping foot inside such a den of iniquity, and now she was having a sexual affair with a man she wasn't even in a relationship with.

She'd never have slept with her ex-boyfriend if she hadn't been utterly convinced that one day—soon—they'd be man and wife. But Phil did not have the looks or the charm of John Fairweather.

No. She couldn't bring a change of clothes. That would be admitting that she planned to do something inappropriate. If something happened spontaneously, that was different. Going into the New Dawn casino with a deliberate intention to have sex with the man she was investigating seemed far more dangerous and inappropriate. Premeditation, after all, was often the difference between manslaughter and murder.

An unplanned crime—or night—of passion was a little different.

She jumped when the phone rang, as if the person calling could read her thoughts.

And maybe they could. "Hi, Mom."

"Hello, sweetheart, are you busy?"

"Yes, very, I'm afraid." She didn't want to get into a conversation that might involve little white lies.

"How long are they going to keep you out there in Massachusetts? It's the church picnic this weekend and I promised you'd run the till. Sally is baking two hundred cupcakes to raise money for the mission in Kenya."

It was Thursday. The thought that in two days she could be back in Ohio, miles away from John, chilled her. "I don't know if I'll be back. I thought I would be, but it keeps getting more complicated. I'm sure you can run the till." She felt a bit guilty. She usually enjoyed helping out at these events. It was fun to see people coming together for a good cause. Now all she could seem to think about was herself and the affair she shouldn't be having.

"I already promised to run the lemonade stand. I suppose Sally's daughter can manage, though. I do wish you were back home. I worry about you being so far away and with the wrong sort of people."

"There's nothing to worry about. They're all quite normal, really. It's a business like any other." She glanced at her face in the mirror, wondering if her nose was getting longer. There was nothing normal about John Fairweather. He was larger than life in every possible way.

"I know people visit casinos of their own free will, but profits from gambling just seem like the wages of sin."

"They're wages like any others when you look at the account books, and that's all I'm here to do. How's Dad doing? Is he taking that new medication the doctor gave him?" Her father's cholesterol had tested high recently. She was so used to taking care of them. If anything, they'd grown even more dependent on her since she moved back home from college, and she wondered how they'd manage without her if she did move out. Especially if she moved away to a different state.

Not that she should even be thinking along those lines since it was very unlikely to happen.

"Your dad is taking his medicine, but he won't stop putting mayonnaise on everything. You'll have to talk some sense into him when you come home. It's odd here without you. The house feels empty and there's no one to do the dishes after dinner."

She had to smile. "I miss you, too. I'm still not sure when I'll be home, but hopefully by next week."

They wished each other goodbye and Constance hung up, then sighed, thinking about the endless nights of putting dishes into the machine and watching alarmist news shows that stretched ahead of her like a lonely highway. Then she shoved her phone in her pocket and headed out the door.

Without a change of underwear.

Constance spent the afternoon stalking the cashiers and wandering around the game rooms. Luckily for her, the New Dawn did not have any kind of middlemen between the customers and the cashiers. Everyone had to bring their own chips to the cashier to turn them into money.

Nothing untoward seemed to be happening at the tables, either. John had told her that the dealers were all experienced professionals, mostly from Atlantic City or Vegas, though he was hoping to train some local people soon.

She walked among the tables watching the customers gamble. People won money. Others lost money. Some won it then lost it. There was nothing that looked fishy. She paused at a roulette table, and watched the croupier spin the wheel.

"Hello, gorgeous." That deep, rich voice in her ear sent a shiver of warm lust to her core.

She resisted the urge to spin around and instead turned very slowly to face John. A smile was already creeping across her face and she worked hard not to let it get too goofy. "Good afternoon, Mr. Fairweather."

"I see you're examining our operations again with that eagle eye of yours. Do you like what you see?"

"Like it? Not so much. I'm still not a fan of gambling." She smiled primly. His own easy expression didn't budge. "And I really should keep my findings confidential at this point, don't you think?"

Now she did see a flicker of surprise in his eyes. "What findings?"

"Any findings I should happen to make." She attempted an air of sphinxlike calm. "I'm not saying I've found anything unusual."

"But you're not saying you haven't." He frowned. "You will tell me if you find anything, won't you? I'd be damn surprised, but I'd want to know right up front."

She hesitated. "My first responsibility is to my client."

"The BIA."

"I'd consider it a personal favor if you'd tell me about anything you find first." His face was now deadly serious.

"I don't think I'm in a position to offer personal favors. I'm here to do a job." This was getting awkward. He obviously thought she'd found something unexpected in the books that she didn't want him to know about it. Still, if she did, she should keep it secret while she investigated, so the casino wouldn't have a chance to cover it all up before she reported back to her client.

She glanced up and saw his uncle Don throw down some chips at a distant roulette table.

"I have no desire to interfere with your performance on the job you've been hired to do. You know that. But honestly, if you find anything amiss, I'd be as keen to know about it as anyone else." His earnest expression preyed on her emotions.

"I'll tell you if I find anything," she whispered. "I really do believe you want everything to be aboveboard. But so far, so good." She smiled. "Though I shouldn't be telling you that."

In the distance, Don swiped up a fistful of chips from the table with a smile and shoved them in his pocket. Darius, who managed the cashiers, had told her that Don gambled. She supposed there was nothing illegal in it. Or was there? This was a perfect instance of where she needed to do her own research rather than asking John about it.

Don Fairweather was now heading toward them, a confident smile on his rather wrinkled face. Constance braced herself. She'd better be on alert to see if she could pick up any information to substantiate or debunk the rumors about him.

"Consorting with the enemy, eh, John?" Don turned to her and winked. "You know I'm just kidding. We welcome the scrutiny of the BIA and all their friends in the media. Life would be dull if everyone just let us go about our business."

"My contact mentioned money-laundering charges against you." She looked at Don and came right out with it. She wanted to hear if his answer would be any less evasive and uninformative than John's. And something about Don's nonchalant attitude pushed her buttons and she wanted to see how he reacted under pressure.

"Load of bull. I used to own a chain of dry cleaners.

We were laundering shirts, not money." His grin challenged her to argue. "As you probably know, they didn't find enough evidence to convict me of anything."

"Don was found not guilty," John cut in. "By a jury of his peers."

"Not that I have any true peers, of course."

"Don is by far the most arrogant of the Fairweathers." John shot a wry glance at Constance.

"Which is saying quite a bit with you around," Don retorted with a crinkly smile. "We keep each other on our toes."

"That we do. One of my favorite things about the New Dawn is that I get to work with family every day." John wrapped his arm around Don. "Sometimes it's a challenge, but maybe that's why I enjoy it so much."

"You'd be bored if life was too easy. And neither of us knew there were so many of us. Some of them barely even knew they had Indian ancestry until John got them excited about this place. Now the kids are begging him to dig up some old songs and dances so they can compete in the big powwows."

John shook his head. "Easier said than done. I vote that they just make up their own. Why does our culture have to be old and historic? Why can't it be fresh and new?"

"Won't win any prizes with that. The judges are traditional. We already have strikes against us because we don't look like most people's idea of an Indian."

"Then people need to change their perceptions, don't they, Constance."

"I suppose they do." How did he always charm her into agreeing with him? She really didn't have an opinion of any kind on the matter. She did think it was sweet how John obviously worked hard to create a sense of community, and was paying a fortune to academics to dig up the

Nissequot tribe's shared history. "And if anyone can do that, it's you."

She blushed, realizing that she'd just praised him in front of his uncle. Don's eyebrows rose a tad. Did he suspect anything between her and John? That would be disastrous. Don Fairweather was something of a loose cannon, aside from his dubious reputation. "I really must get back to the offices."

"I'll ride up with you." John's low voice gave the innocent offer a suggestive tone.

"Actually, I need to get something from my car first." She didn't want Don to see them disappearing together.

John wouldn't tell Don about their liaison, would he? She really didn't know. Don was his uncle and they were obviously close. She reminded herself that she barely knew John at all. She nodded to them primly and hustled toward the lobby. She didn't actually need anything from her car but she'd fiddle around in there for a minute or so. Anything to get away from John's dark, seductive gaze.

She futzed around with her bag on the passenger seat for a moment, then pulled it out and closed the car door. She turned toward the casino and gasped when she found John right in front of her.

"I'm not letting you sneak off."

"I wasn't trying to sneak off." She lifted her chin. "I was getting my phone charger."

"Oh." His smile suggested that he knew it was a ruse. "You looked like you were running away from something."

"Your uncle Don doesn't know about…us, does he?"

John shrugged. "I haven't told him anything. Even if he figured it out, he'd be discreet. He's got enough skeletons in his own closet that he's not going to throw open the door to anyone else's."

Why was that not at all reassuring? "I don't think we should walk back in together."

"Why not?" He looked a little put out. "I'm the CEO of the place. I hardly think it's inappropriate of me to escort the forensic accountant up to the offices." He leaned in and whispered in her ear, "Even if I do know how she looks without her clothes on."

Constance sucked in a breath. Heat flushed her entire body and she wasn't sure if it was embarrassment or lust. It didn't really matter. Neither was at all helpful right now.

"You're incorrigible." Luckily there was no one else around.

"I know. It's an affliction. Do you think you can cure me?"

"I doubt it. I also have no intention of trying." She shifted her bag higher on her shoulder. "And I have work to do."

"Let's go." He led the way, then waited for her to catch up so they could enter the lobby together. She held her chin high, self-conscious as she walked with him through the public space. The staff all knew who she was by now. Did they suspect anything? She felt so different than she had even yesterday, it was hard to imagine that she could still look the same from the outside.

When they reached the office, John ushered her in, then followed her and closed the door. She heard the lock click and felt his arm reach around her waist and her backside crushed up against his hard form.

"Constance, you're making me crazy."

She tried to hide her smile. "Maybe you were crazy already."

"I don't know what you've done to me."

"I can't imagine that I've done anything." His big

hand splayed over her belly, where all kinds of sensations churned. "I'm just trying to do my job."

"And I keep distracting you." His lips brushed her neck and heat flickered low inside her.

"Yes. Very much so."

"I think you needed some distraction." His low voice sent a rumble of desire to her toes.

"So I'll be unable to properly investigate your books? You'll make me think you're trying to hide something."

"Maybe there is something I'm trying to hide." His voice contained more than a hint of suggestion, and she felt his erection jostle against her. She was slightly appalled by how arousing that was. What had happened to her since she met John Fairweather? It was as though a switch had turned on inside her. Now energy coursed through her veins whenever she was around him. Her mind strayed in previously forbidden directions and her body ached to do all kinds of things that she knew were wrong.

"What are we doing?" she asked in a half whisper.

His mouth played below her ear, heating her skin. "I think I'm kissing your neck."

"This is foolish."

"I won't argue with you." He went back to kissing her neck. Her nipples were starting to tingle.

"So shouldn't we stop?"

His mouth worked its way up to her ear and he nibbled softly on her earlobe, which sent a surprising surge of sensation to her core. "Definitely not."

He spun her around and kissed her full on the mouth. Her lips parted to welcome him and she felt her arms wrap enthusiastically around him without her permission. They kissed for a solid ten minutes, until she was in a thoroughly befuddled state. Then he excused himself with a polite nod and left her all alone, in a state of agonizing arousal, with nothing but ledger books for company.

She stared at the door. What a nerve! Now he had her all worked up and he'd waltzed off? He hadn't even said where he was going or when he'd be back. How could she work now that he'd left her with blood pounding in every part of her body other than her brain?

She glanced at her watch and saw that it was nearly seven o'clock. She'd wasted most of the afternoon seeing nothing downstairs. Except for Don Fairweather swiping those chips off the table.

Of course she'd seen him put chips down to bet, so nothing truly suspicious had happened, but wasn't it rather a conflict of interest for him to gamble in the tribe's own casino? He wasn't involved in the day-to-day operations on the floor. He did publicity and booked the bands, but he was obviously fairly intimate with all the other workers. She'd noticed his jovial exchanges with at least half a dozen employees on the floor. Which was hardly proof of wrongdoing.

She heaved a sigh of relief to find that thinking about Don helped dissipate the fog of passion that John had left her in. She turned to the computer and had a look through the entries from a year ago. There was no point in looking at new data, since everyone knew she was here so any would-be crooks would be on their best behavior. As usual everything seemed to add up.

Often with forensic accounting she wasn't looking for overt proof of wrongdoing. White-collar criminals were usually smart and knew how to cover their tracks. She had to look closely to find tiny holes or data that was just a little different from the norm. Then she at least had a clue for somewhere to stick in her shovel and start digging. So far she'd had no luck. Every time she'd thought she found an interesting anomaly, it had turned out to be a dead end.

On instinct she decided to look for internal records of tribal members gambling. They were easy enough to find in the casino databases, which were very well organized and clearly labeled, probably by John himself. Don wasn't the only member who gambled, but he was by far the heaviest gambler. Someone called Mona Lester had some losses, and an Anna Martin had some small winnings, but Don had won more than fifty thousand dollars last year. Could he be up to something, or was he just lucky?

The door clicked open and John appeared again. She closed the spreadsheet window with a flash of guilt. Which was ridiculous. He knew she was here to dig into the files, so she was hardly going behind his back. Still, it felt wrong to kiss a man then go looking for fraud in his own computer system.

One more reason why this whole affair was a big mistake.

He closed the door behind him and leaned against it. His sleek dark suit did nothing to conceal the raw masculinity of his body. Especially not now that she'd seen it naked. "You're coming to my house for dinner."

"You mean your suite." Her response seemed easier than choosing to accept or decline his invitation. Not an invitation, really. More of a command.

"No, I mean my house. I'm just living in the suite while I renovate the old farmhouse. The kitchen's finished, so I have everything I need to make dinner for you."

"You can cook?"

"Absolutely."

She blinked, not sure what to believe. Was there anything he couldn't do? "I can't really say no, then, can I?"

"Of course not." He offered a hand to help her from her seat behind the desk.

She must be out of her mind. But, he could cook? That was pretty irresistible. And she could go back to her hotel right after dinner. "I'll drive in my car." Then she could take off any time she wanted.

"Sure. You can follow me."

The road to his house was long and winding, an old farm road that led past his grandparents' new house and through fields dotted with grazing cattle. Gnarled apple trees lined the drive and framed the austere form of John's white farmhouse. A new cedar-shake roof gleamed gold in the lowering sun and stickers still ornamented the shiny new windows. A Dumpster filled with construction debris and a cement mixer were among the signs that a major renovation was still in progress.

"We stripped it right back to the old post-and-beam framing, and added stud walls and insulation. There's almost nothing left of the original house, but it's starting to look like it used to in its heyday. All the major work is done. Now they're reinstalling the original woodwork. I should be back living here in a month or so."

"It looks lovely." She was surprised that a notorious bachelor like John would even want a big old house when he could be catered to by staff at his own luxury hotel.

"It's coming together really well. I can't wait to move in. I'm going to get a dog."

"What kind?"

"I don't know yet. Something big. And cute. I'll adopt it from a shelter."

"That's a great idea. I've always wanted a dog."

"Why don't you get one?"

"I need to move out of my parents' house first. My mom doesn't like them."

He nodded. He must think it pathetic that she still lived at home with her parents at age twenty-seven. She needed to put moving out at the top of her goals for the coming year.

They walked up solid stone steps to the front door, which was still stripped bare of paint. John opened it and ushered her in. She glanced around his inner sanctum, taking in all the authentic details he'd had lovingly preserved.

"This house was built in 1837 by one of my ancestors. He and his sons handcrafted a lot of the woodwork themselves."

She stroked a turned cherry bannister. "This must have been quite a labor of love before power tools became common."

"All the more reason to restore it to its original beauty." He led her into a bright kitchen with ivory cabinets and big center island. "Do you like shrimp?"

"Love it."

"Good, because I've had it marinating since this morning."

"You knew you were going to ask me over?"

"Of course."

His arrogance should have been annoying. "What if I said I didn't like shrimp? Or I was allergic."

He shot her a cheeky smile. "I've got some chicken prepared as well."

"You're ready for anything, aren't you?"

"I try to be."

He grilled the shrimp and some corn on the cob outdoors, and they ate it with an elaborate salad they made together of feta cheese and pear tossed with spring greens. The million-dollar view from his bluestone patio looked over pastures and rolling wooded hills. Constance couldn't remember a time she'd been anywhere so beautiful. Her own drab environs in an unprepossessing part of Cleveland were depressing by comparison. Yet soon she'd be back there, looking off the back porch over the weedy garden, remembering this delicious dinner and her dangerously charming host.

Dark clouds were gathering along the horizon as the sun disappeared behind the trees. Raindrops spotted the patio as they brought the plates back inside, and by the time they loaded them in the dishwasher, rain was pounding on the darkened windows.

While John brewed the fresh-ground coffee, thunderclaps boomed overhead. "You'd better wait until this stops." Anticipation shimmered in his gaze.

She reached into her bag. "Let me check the satellite images on my phone to see how big the storm looks."

"I already did. It's going to continue all night."

Eight

Had John somehow planned this storm along with everything else about this evening? He seemed so vastly in control of his life and nearly everyone else's that it might just be possible. She wasn't a pawn here. She had free will. "I'm sure I can drive in it."

"I won't allow it." He towered over her in the dimly lit kitchen.

"What makes you think you can allow it or not allow it? You're not my boss."

"But I am concerned about your safety. These back roads can wash out in this kind of storm. Some of the worst messes I see as a volunteer firefighter are one-car accidents where someone tried to drive at night in the wrong weather. It's too hard to see the road when you're out in the woods in rainy darkness."

"I suppose you do have a point," she muttered. "But I can't sleep with you."

"I believe we've passed that milestone already."

"I know, but that was a one-time, spur-of-the-moment thing. If I stay over again…"

"It'll mean you actually like me." His teeth flashed in a wicked grin.

She had no idea how to respond to that. Especially since

it was true. "I don't know why I like you. You're insufferably arrogant."

"You find that refreshing because you're used to dealing with wimps."

"That's not true at all." *I'm not used to dealing with anyone.* She couldn't believe she'd actually admitted to John that she hadn't even been on a single date since she broke up with her college boyfriend.

"Then maybe I'm just likable." He crossed the kitchen in two strides and placed his hands on her hips. Heat flared between them. His gentle but insistent kiss left her speechless, and she noticed how her treacherous fingers were already sliding lower to the curve of his backside. How did he do this to her?

She didn't want to tell him she liked him. He might take it the wrong way and think she wanted some kind of real relationship with him. That was impossible, of course.

She knew that. Which was why she shouldn't be here kissing a man who had no honorable intentions toward her.

Nevertheless, she found herself kissing him back with passion that that flowed from somewhere deep inside her. This was the kind of thing they'd warned her about in Sunday school. That her parents tut-tutted over when other girls from her neighborhood had affairs that quickly fizzled out, sometimes leaving them pregnant. They thought you shouldn't even kiss someone until there was a ring or a promise in the picture.

Constance had neither, and yet her fingers now tugged at John's tie and the buttons on his shirt.

"Let's go upstairs." He didn't wait for an answer but swept her along with his powerful arm around her waist. He kissed her neck with each step, caressed her backside as she walked ahead of him. Under his admiring gaze and tender touch she felt unbelievably desirable. She even had a swing in her step she'd never felt before. Being with John Fairweather was doing something very strange to her mind and body.

"This is my room." She walked into an impressive chamber with a beamed cathedral ceiling. A big hand-hewn bed gave the room a masculine air. Framed maps decorated the walls, and she peered at one as they went past. "Those are the historical survey maps of our land and the town around it." They were all different. She could see the territory marked out for the Nissequot shrinking as the maps leaped over the decades. By the early part of the twentieth century, the word *Nissequot* wasn't even there and it was marked as Fairweather Farm.

"They were trying to squeeze you out of existence."

"Almost worked, too."

He wrapped his arms around her from behind as she stood in front of the most recent map. It was from the previous year and showed the Nissequot territory proudly marked in green, expanded and with the casino buildings at its center.

"What's the blue area?"

"That's what we're planning to buy next. Even that won't take us all the way back to our colonial-era hunting grounds, but it'll give us room to grow."

Her heart filled with pride at all he'd accomplished. Which didn't really make sense, since she had nothing to do with it and he wasn't hers to begin with.

"Now, where were we?" He spun her slowly around, sliding his hands along the curve of her waist. The thunder still rumbled outside and rain hammered against the glass of the windows, but it all faded to nothing when his lips touched hers. Her eyes slid closed and she leaned into him, enjoying the closeness she hadn't even known she craved. Lost deep in the kiss, it wasn't until she opened her eyes to undo his belt buckle that she realized all the lights had gone out.

"Have we lost power?"

"Looks that way." He kissed her forehead. "We're generating plenty of our own electricity, so I don't think we need it."

She laughed. "Shouldn't we at least call the electric company?"

"Nah. They can tell when we lose power. The casino and hotel have backup generators, so they won't miss a beat."

He'd taken off her jacket and undone her blouse, and now he unzipped her skirt so it fell to the floor. The black velvet darkness felt very intimate. She managed to get his belt unhooked and his pants and shirt off, which involved some giggling and fumbling. Then they made their way to the soft surface of the bed.

He held her tight as they rolled together, pressing their bodies into the mattress and each other. She loved the heaviness of him, how big he was. When she was on top she kissed his face all over, then eased down to his shoulders and neck, leaving a trail of kisses. She wanted to explore his body, and the total darkness made her bold.

She liked the roughness of the hair on his chest. There wasn't much of it, just enough to create an interesting and masculine texture. She traced it lower, to where she could feel his hardness waiting for her. She let her tongue explore his erection, turning off any whispers in her mind of how this was indulgent and sinful. She loved the way he moved in response to everything she did, aroused to the point where he couldn't keep still. John groaned softly as she took him into her mouth and sucked, then let her tongue play about the tip of his penis.

She'd never done this before. Never even thought about

it! She enjoyed the control she had over him. She could feel the desire, the passion that racked his strong body.

"Oh, Constance. We need to find a condom."

She laughed, so aroused she could hardly think. Thank goodness he was more sensible than she. "I love how you're so responsible."

"It goes with being a leader of the tribe. I don't want to create any new members except on purpose." He chuckled and she heard him groping around in the darkness, opening a door in the nightstand. It reminded her that she was not the first woman to come to his bed. She wouldn't be the last, either.

But as he rolled the condom on in the dark, she didn't seem to care. Constance was so aroused that she took him inside her effortlessly, welcoming him into her body. Still on top, she moved slowly, experimenting with the sensations she created in herself and in him. As pressure built inside her she moved faster, letting the feelings wash over her and surprise her as her body did what it wanted.

John pulled her toward him and rolled them over again so he was on top, then he kissed her softly and started a different rhythm that soon had her gasping aloud and moaning his name.

She'd never done that before, either.

He took her almost to the brink, then pulled back, slowing down and kissing and caressing her until she felt she might burst. She tried to urge him with her hips, but he was too heavy, and only chuckled at her attempts to drive the motion. "Impatient!" he scolded her. "Everything in due time." He moved very slowly and quietly, layering kisses over her ears and neck, heightening the already intense reactions taking place inside her.

She was so aroused that she could barely breathe by the time he finally brought them both to a blistering climax that lit up the darkness with an explosion of inner electricity she'd never even dreamed was possible.

"I saw fireworks," she gasped when she could finally speak again.

"Good," was all he replied, so obnoxiously confident that she wanted to slap him—or hug him. She chose the latter.

John buried his face in her hair. They lay side by side, wrapped in each other. This seduction had taken him by surprise and it just kept gathering steam.

He hadn't realized that looking past her glasses into those hazel eyes would put him under her quiet spell. Now he didn't want Constance to leave at all. The power was back on and a soft light illuminated the room.

"Did you put your glasses somewhere safe?"

"They're on the bedside table." Her soft voice was a balm to his spirit.

"Good. I didn't remember you taking them off and I don't want them to get broken."

"That's sweet of you."

Yeah. She was bringing out the sweet in him. He wanted to cherish her and take care of her. He loved to feel her relaxing in his arms. Letting go of the prickly armor she'd used to hold him at bay. It was magic to feel her opening up and exploring her own sensuality—and driving him half-insane in the bargain.

He kissed her cheek. "You're something else, Constance Allen."

"I'm certainly something else from who I thought I was. There have been a lot of surprises for me here in Massachusetts."

"You're surprised that I'm not the greedy crook the media make me out to be."

"I had no preconceptions about you. I strive to be entirely open-minded. It's essential in my work. If you go in with opinions, it will skew how you perceive the data."

"You had no idea you'd succumb to my famous charms."

"Now that is true." Her eyes sparkled with humor. "I'm still not sure what the heck I'm doing in your arms."

"Relaxing."

"It's not very relaxing knowing that if my boss—or anyone else—found out I'd be fired and probably lose my accounting credentials."

"That's why you're not thinking about that part." He didn't want her to go back to her job and Ohio. He wanted her to stay here.

The thought struck him like a bolt of lightning. The thunder rolling outside echoed a storm that raged quietly in his heart. He was falling for Constance Allen. "Where are you hoping to go next in your career?"

"I'd like to achieve partner eventually. At least, I suppose I would. That's the logical peak of my career. If I manage not to destroy it between now and then."

"Have you ever wanted to do anything else?" Possibilities blossomed in his imagination. She could manage the casino's accounts. After a reasonable cooling-off period from her assignment, of course. Their personal relationship would seem to develop naturally out of her employment at the casino.

Uh-oh. His feelings for Constance were making him creative.

"Not really. When I was younger I wanted to be a teacher, but I grew out of that. I'm better with numbers than people."

He cocked his head. "I can see you being a teacher. And I think you're just fine with people."

"I don't know. What if the kids didn't listen to me?"

Every now and then, when she was bored out of her mind with a particular project, she wondered if she'd made the wrong choice.

"Numbers don't talk back."

"Not often, anyway." Soft and warm, she lay still against his chest. She no longer seemed ready to run away. "Though I'm always hoping that they'll yell at me. Especially in a forensic investigation."

"Like the one you're doing now." He stroked her hair.

"Exactly. I can't believe I'm lying in your arms when I'm going to be combing through your books looking for fraud tomorrow."

"Surely you've seen all you need to see by now. It's hard to prove there's absolutely no wrongdoing, but at what point do you call it quits?"

She stiffened slightly. "When the BIA tells me to."

"They still aren't satisfied?"

"They just want me to be thorough. I'm sure they're as anxious as you are to have everything check out so they can forget about the whole thing."

"I hope so. They could put us right out of business if they had a mind to. Believe me, I have no interest in doing anything that isn't entirely aboveboard. I know we're under scrutiny and that our work can stand up to it."

"Then you have nothing to worry about. I'm sure they'll get bored with paying my hourly rate soon."

"I hope not." He held her tight. "Or I might have to convince you to quit and move here." There, he'd said it. He was clearly losing his sanity, but it was a relief to get it off his chest.

She stilled. "Very funny."

"You think I'm kidding?"

"I know you're kidding."

"Don't be so sure. I like you." He kissed her on the nose. "And you like me, too."

She laughed. "I do. But not enough to throw away my life and career to prolong a steamy affair with you." He heard an odd note in her voice. Sadness. She was already mourning the end of their relationship, even as they lay nestled in each other's arms.

"It doesn't have to end." His voice emerged a little gruffer than he'd intended.

"I suppose you could always move to Ohio." She raised one of her slim brows.

"That wouldn't be ideal."

"See? It's impossible. We have our separate lives already planned out and this is just a big mistake that we couldn't seem to avoid." She said it so seriously that he laughed.

"Speak for yourself. I don't consider this to be a mistake at all. This is the best evening I can remember having. Followed closely by last night."

"You must have a short memory, that's all." She closed her eyes for a second, as if enjoying a thought, then opened them. "You'll have forgotten all about me in a month. In six months you won't even remember my name."

"How could I forget a name like Constance? I can't believe you won't let me call you Connie."

"Knowing you, I can't believe you haven't started doing it anyway, regardless of what I think."

"I'm more sensitive than you take me for." He caressed her soft cheek. "In fact, I can be quite soft hearted."

It was the honest truth. Which he usually kept to himself. He'd prided himself on keeping his emotions in check for a long time. Something about Constance made him want to let his guard down. He knew she wasn't interested in his money, or his notoriety, or even his dashing good looks. To appeal to her he'd have to be honest and prove to her that he wasn't the hard-hearted lothario she believed him to be.

Was he really trying to convince her to stay here? His logical mind argued against it but something deep in his gut told him that if he let her go he'd regret it, possibly for the rest of his life.

"I didn't bring a change of underwear."

"We sell some nice panties in the shop." He grinned. "I can pick some up for you."

"No! That'll just get the staff wondering who they're for. I'll go back to my hotel first thing in the morning. Don't let me sleep in, okay?"

"I'll wake you. Though it will cause me pain to tug you from your dreams." He sounded pretty sappy. For some reason around Constance that felt okay. He could tell she liked it. She had a tiny smile across her mouth and her eyes were closed. She looked utterly relaxed and at peace. Which, considering the circumstances and her personality, was quite something.

He could easily imagine her lying here in his bed, in his arms, for a long time to come. Getting to that point, however, was going to take some careful management of what could be a very explosive situation. He regretted joking around with Don about flirting with her. Though maybe that would help throw him off the scent. He didn't want Don to know about any of this until the time was right, which would likely be months from now, as his uncle could have a big mouth.

Constance Fairweather. The name had an old-fashioned sound that was strangely appealing to him.

Her breathing slowed as she slipped into sleep. All her resistance had evaporated and she was totally comfortable and relaxed here, with him. Of course her family probably wouldn't be too thrilled about him taking her several states away, but they could easily move here and he could build them a nice house like the one his grandparents lived in. He'd learned from experience that all obstacles could be overcome with the right planning and some patience. She liked him, he could tell. There was no way she would be here if she didn't. And he liked her.

So what could go wrong?

Constance was awakened by John's gentle kiss on her cheek. She blinked and took in the sight of his handsome face, wondering if she was still dreaming.

"Good morning, gorgeous. I made us breakfast. You've got plenty of time to eat before hitting the road to your hotel."

"Okay." She must be dreaming. And why wake up?

They ate a feast of fresh fruit and scrambled eggs with toast, drank freshly brewed coffee and juice and chatted about their childhoods, which had both been somewhat outside the mainstream in their own way. As the hands on the vintage wall clock headed toward eight o'clock, she found herself reluctant to leave.

Sitting here chatting with him felt utterly natural. He was just so easy to talk to, and so warm and such a good host. He was spoiling her for all other men. Not that any other men were knocking on her door, but it was going to be hard to find someone whose company she enjoyed as much as John's.

Of course, there was plenty wrong with him. He was far too good-looking. She didn't value looks at all. In fact, they tended to make her assume someone was arrogant and conceited—which in John's case was entirely correct. Yet since his cocky attitude was justified by his impressive competence, somehow it seemed appropriate.

She knew he was a notorious playboy. She was just another notch on his hand-hewn bedpost. One in a long line of women, and probably less enticing than most. Once she went back to Ohio, she'd never see him again and very soon there would be another woman in his bed and sitting here at his kitchen table.

The thoughts made her gut clench with sadness. Which was exactly why she shouldn't have let herself fall into this…liaison in the first place. He could easily add it to his list of pleasurable experiences and move on. She didn't have a list of pleasurable experiences and this was going to stand out as one of the most amazing, unexpected and wonderful events of her life.

Fantastic.

John's phone kept making noises, and eventually he picked it up and looked at his messages. "Sounds like the media's still making noise about Don today."

"Do you think he's done anything wrong?" she couldn't help asking.

"No." He answered quickly. "He's made some…ill-advised choices in the past, but I know he wouldn't do anything to jeopardize what we've built here. He likes people to think he's a bad boy. He thinks it's a cool image. Doesn't bother me. All publicity is good publicity to a certain extent. We're still new enough that a lot of people haven't been here yet and you never know what will get them off the couch."

"Don sounds like quite a character."

"Oh, he is. Sometimes he drives me nuts, but he was the first person to jump on board when I came up with the idea for this place. My grandparents thought it was impossible."

"Why?"

"Too big. Too bold. How can you take a tired dairy farm in the middle of nowhere and turn it into a thriving attraction? But we're not the first, and we won't be the last. Don had faith in my ability to pull it off and he's worked hard to make it happen."

"I can tell you have a lot of affection for him."

"I do. He's my uncle. And under his flashy exterior he's a big softy." John smiled.

Oh, dear. He was being adorable again. Couldn't he be a jerk just to make it easier for her to go back home? "I'd better get going."

"I'll lead the way."

John watched Constance head for the highway to her hotel, then returned to the offices. Don was in the lobby, chatting with one of the desk clerks. He brightened at the sight of John. "Ready for breakfast?"

"I grabbed something at home."

"What'd you do that for?"

"No reason." Don would die laughing if he knew. "Just hungry, that's all." The truth. His night had been rather more athletic than usual. And he still had a distinct spring in his step. Constance was full of intriguing surprises.

"Come have coffee with me then. We can glare at any reporters and scare them off."

"It's usually better to just answer their questions with a smile." Why were reporters still sniffing around? Nothing had happened lately to arouse their suspicion. "Have you seen any today?"

"I had a phone call this morning asking questions about your lady friend."

John stiffened. "Constance?" He realized he might have revealed too much. "Ms. Allen from the BIA?"

Don nodded. "Somehow word got out that they're looking into our books. I suppose they're going on the theory that where there's smoke there's probably a fire."

"But there isn't."

"You know that, and I know that, and we just have to wait for them to realize that."

"Hmm." The press couldn't possibly suspect anything between him and Constance, could they? That would be bad, for her and for him and for the casino. Don didn't seem to suspect anything.

"She good in bed?"

John froze. "Who?"

Don nudged him. "You can't fool me. I've known you since you were two feet high. I can see the way you look at her."

"I have no idea what you're talking about." John maintained a calm demeanor but inside he was starting to sweat. Was his newfound passion for Constance really so obvious? It was essential to keep it a secret until her investigation was over and the results had been announced—for her sake, if not his own.

"Miss Constance Allen, forensic accountant. I bet she's a freak under that conservative suit."

"You're disgusting. Who do we have booked to perform in September?"

"I just booked Jimmy Cliff. I'm working on Celine Dion."

"You keep working. I'm heading up to the office." John headed toward the elevators, blood pumping.

Right now he was ready for Constance to leave.

Not because he didn't want to see her again. Because he wanted to be done with all the secrecy and subterfuge, and that couldn't end until she was no longer investigating him. He needed her to go back to Ohio, wrap up her assignment, and then they could start over again.

And that couldn't happen soon enough.

* * *

Back at her hotel, Constance showered and returned some phone calls. It was Friday and the perfect day to pack up and leave, but for some reason she had a feeling she'd no longer be irritated by a request to stay for a few more days. She wasn't ready to say goodbye to John. In fact she was secretly hoping they'd get to spend at least one more night together.

She knew such thoughts were possibly signs of appalling moral degeneration, but she couldn't remember ever having this much fun with anyone before, and she wasn't ready to go back to her humdrum existence yet.

She called the BIA with considerable trepidation. She was starting to feel like a total fraud as far as they were concerned. If they knew what she was up to with John, they'd fire her firm on the spot and probably sue her for damaging their reputation. She decided to mention the closest thing to a discovery that she'd come across. "Don Fairweather gambles in the casino. He had substantial winnings last year. More than fifty thousand."

"Did he pay taxes on his winnings?"

"I'm not sure. I haven't looked at the individual tribal members' tax returns."

"Request them, and take a look."

"Which members?" Was she going to have to look into the returns of every low-level staffer? She felt like rubbing her hands together. That would take several days.

She didn't want to look into John's, though. That seemed far too personal.

"Anyone who's been gambling," Nicola replied. "You'll quickly find out who's honest. And request returns for the key players, including John Fairweather. Take a look at income, expenses, deductions. Poke around a bit. Look into at least five people in total."

"Aren't tax returns confidential? What if they won't allow me access?"

"Then I'll secure a subpoena."

Constance felt jumpy and anxious as she pulled back into the casino parking lot. Personal income tax records? Many people didn't even like sharing the information with their spouse. She took the elevator up to the offices, hoping John wasn't there. It was awkward seeing him in the professional context of the office after what had gone on between them. She always felt her blood heat at the first glimpse of him, then that embarrassing slow smile wanting to creep across her face. And she'd rather request his tax records in a polite text or email than have to look into his eyes while she asked to pry into his personal business.

Of course he was there. Larger than life and twice as handsome. He was talking to a man she recognized from the cashier's office as she approached, but he dismissed him with a nod. The twinkle in his eyes warred with his cool and professional demeanor.

"Hi, Constance."

She straightened her shoulders and tried to affect a disinterested expression. "Good morning." As if she was saying it for the first time.

"Good morning. I trust you slept well." His low voice caused awareness to ripple through her. They walked toward his office together.

"Very well, thank you." He should know. He'd had to wake her up from her blissful slumber. She kept her voice clipped. "Can I speak to you in private?"

"Of course." They took the elevator up to his office. She could feel his curiosity heating the atmosphere as they rode up in silence. She did her best to avoid his glance, afraid of the effect it might have on her.

She took a deep breath. "My contact at the BIA has

requested that I look into the personal tax returns of several key people."

His expression darkened. "Who?"

"You." She spat it right out. She'd chosen people from different departments and in different stages of life so there would be some variety, and she'd included the three gamblers. "Your uncle Don, Paul McGee, Mona Lester, Susan Cummings, Anna Martin and Darius Carter."

"Darius? He's just a kid. He barely even pays taxes."

She shrugged. She'd picked him because he held a key role in the day-to-day running of the casino. "Shall I speak to each person individually?"

"Why these people?"

"They were chosen more or less at random." She didn't want to go into detail. It really wasn't his business. He must have read her reluctance because he paused for a moment, but didn't ask more questions.

"I'll talk to them." His brow had furrowed.

"Do you think any of them will object?"

"I'll make sure they don't. Besides, we all filed the taxes already, so what is there to hide?"

"Exactly."

"I'll have them all for you by the end of the day."

"Much appreciated." Phew. That was easy. As long as none of the individuals objected, of course.

"I want to kiss you." His voice was ripe with suggestion.

"I don't think that's a good idea." Her own voice was barely a whisper. Her lips twitched to do exactly what he'd suggested. "I have work to do."

"So do I. But that doesn't stop me wanting you."

"You're trouble."

"I can't argue with you. I certainly seem to be trouble where you're concerned." They'd reached his office. "Though I don't have any regrets."

He closed the door. They kissed for a solid five minutes, tongues tangling and biting each other's lips until their breath came in ragged gasps.

"I used to be a dignified professional, I'll have you know," she stammered when their lips finally parted.

"I used to be a sane man. Since you showed up here everything has gone out the window." Cool and calm as always, in his dark gray suit and pale blue shirt he looked the picture of sanity. Of course he was probably just pretending to be besotted with her. Or maybe even allowing himself to be as a temporary condition. He'd be over her before she even drove across the Ohio state line. "I hope it will take a while to go through all our returns."

"I hope not. It's embarrassing and totally unprofessional, but I really don't want to find anything wrong here." She couldn't believe she'd confessed that to him.

"Uh-oh. I hope I'm not compromising your professional integrity." His wicked grin warmed her as his big hands squeezed her hips gently.

"Nothing could compromise my professional integrity. Believe me, if I found something, I'd report it."

"I love that about you, Constance. I bet everyone always knows where they stand with you."

"I used to think so. I'm sure my employer would be rather surprised if they knew you were squeezing my butt right now."

He slid his hand back up to her waist with a rueful expression. "True. But since our intimacy doesn't affect your professional integrity, they really shouldn't mind at all."

"Perhaps not, but I'm sure they would." She straightened his pale yellow tie, which had gotten crooked. "Now you and I should at least pretend to do some work. Preferably in separate rooms, as we don't seem to be too professional anymore when we're in the same space."

"All right, Constance. I'll see you later, and I'll have everyone go home at lunch and pick up their tax returns."

"Perfect." Could it really be that easy? "And I might need to speak to each of them individually after I've had a chance to look over the paperwork. I might even need to look at their personal banking records to make sure everything adds up." She held her breath. No one wanted a total stranger looking into their personal finances. On the other hand, it was one of her favorite things to request, since the person's reaction told you a lot about how honest they were.

"I'll warn them. And I consider myself warned." He winked. He didn't look at all worried, which was quite a relief.

She had one more question for him. One she already knew the answer to. "Do any of the tribal members gamble in the casino?"

"I don't do it myself and I prefer that other employees don't. Besides, they know better than anyone that over time the house always wins. Don likes to play a little, but no one else gambles regularly. Believe me, I keep close tabs on all our employees, especially the younger ones."

"Does Don win?"

"He says he does." John winked. "Whether he's telling the truth is a whole different story. We do keep files on employee gambling, though."

"Could I take a look at those?" No need to mention that she'd already seen them and knew Don had big winnings. It would be interesting to see from Don's tax return whether he was claiming them. She felt a little guilty pretending to be totally in the dark, but at least now she felt as though she was actually doing her job.

"Of course." He leaned over the laptop on the desk and tapped a few keys. The file she'd found by herself popped up. "You won't find my name in there."

"I'm glad that you don't gamble."

"Me, too. It's much safer being the house than trying to beat it."

He didn't even glance at the file, so confident that the records were all aboveboard and would speak for themselves. She loved how honorable John was. Another kiss on the lips and a warm hug left her dizzy. Her heart ached as the door closed behind him. If parting from him now hurt her even a little, how was she going to feel when he was gone for good?

Nine

John didn't invite her over that night. She didn't know whether to be relieved or disappointed as she drove back to her hotel, the employees' tax returns sitting on her passenger seat. He probably had some kind of meeting. Or something important to do. Or bigger plans. It was Friday night, after all.

If she had a life she'd drive back to Ohio for the weekend. But it made more sense to stay here, save the gas money and bill more hours.

For dinner, she ate a Chinese chicken salad and drank a Diet Coke at her hotel room desk while she watched the news. The pile of tax returns now stared at her from the end of her bed. She was literally afraid to look at them. Normally the prospect of delving into freshly unearthed personal papers filled her with unreasonable glee. Now it just made her nervous about confronting her own principles.

What if she found something in John's tax return? Excessive write-offs or under-reporting of taxes owed, maybe. She'd be duty bound to report her findings, or even any suspicions. Should she tell him first, so he'd have a chance to explain? She'd told him she would, but that would go in the face of everything she'd learned about forensic accounting. Never give people a chance to cover their tracks.

He hadn't said anything at all about whether it was easy or hard to convince the employees to hand over their returns. Maybe they respected him so much they'd do anything he asked. She'd expected at least someone to put up a fight. So far it was all going too smoothly. For reasons she couldn't put her finger on, that made her nervous.

She picked his tax return off the pile first with trembling fingers. His income was exorbitant, of course, but most of it was from personal investments that had nothing whatsoever to do with New Dawn. He'd only paid himself a salary of one hundred thousand from the casino and hotel. That impressed her. He'd taken plenty of personal deductions and travel expenses, but nothing out of the ordinary. His return looked similar to many she'd seen belonging to successful company owners and high-level executives. He'd paid a great deal in taxes, mostly capital-gains tax, so the government should be quite happy to have John Fairweather as a taxpayer. After several hours combing through the schedules, she heaved a sigh of relief and moved on.

Darius's and Anna's returns reflected their modest incomes and were totally uncomplicated, and they'd both received a small amount of money back when they filed. Anna had reported her small gambling winnings, so there was no problem there. Mona had gotten divorced in the middle of the year, so her return was more elaborate, but still nothing to arouse suspicion.

She left Don's for last. It was almost as thick as John's and she soon discovered that he actually earned more than John from New Dawn. No doubt it was John's way of keeping a senior family member happy. Still, the salary was far from outrageous for a senior executive at such a profitable enterprise, and Don had paid taxes at a high rate and taken fairly reasonable deductions.

But as she combed through the schedules, she saw nothing at all about proceeds from personal gambling. Her Spidey-sense tingled with alarm. Normally this was a good feeling that she was about to earn her keep and justify her employment at a top accounting firm. But right now it came with an uncomfortable sense of foreboding. She went through the return again. Still no sign of any winnings or losses. Since the casino workers openly admitted to him gambling, and she'd seen him do it with her own eyes, it was clearly an omission. Even though table games like roulette and blackjack didn't require that the casino submit Form W2-G to the IRS, the gambler was certainly required to declare winnings and she'd seen the records detailing Don's fifty thousand dollars in profits.

Her phone rang and she almost jumped out of her skin. It was Lynn from work. What was she doing calling on a Friday night? "Hi." Constance hoped she could get her off the phone quickly.

"I hope you're back in Cleveland because you're the only person I know who will go see the new Disney movie with me."

Constance couldn't help laughing. "I would love to see it, but I'm still in Massachusetts."

"Why didn't you drive home for the weekend? I guess you can't bring yourself to leave the sexy casino boss."

"What? You're crazy. I barely even see him." She realized she'd spoken too fast and too loud.

"Oh, boy. I did hit a nerve. I always knew you'd be interested if the right man came along."

"You're talking nonsense. I could care less about John Fairweather."

Lynn laughed. "Don't you mean *couldn't* care less? If you could care less then it means you care quite a bit."

"You know what I mean." Constance leaped to her feet and paced in her small hotel room. "I'm only interested in his financial data." Now she was lying to her closest friend. "Which is checking out fine."

"What a bummer. I was hoping for a dramatic exposé and scandal that would lead to a big bonus for you next spring."

"I'm just doing my job. I have no expectations of any kind when I look into a company's books."

"I know, I know. It's just so much more interesting when you find information that someone was trying to hide."

Now would be the perfect time to mention the telling absence of gambling data on Don Fairweather's tax return. Yet she kept quiet. She'd promised to tell John about anything she found. It chilled her to realize that she felt more loyalty to John than to her own firm. Still, she wouldn't lie or cover anything up. As soon as she'd told John, she'd report back to her firm, and to the BIA.

Hopefully since it was just a personal matter, and not to do with the casino itself, it would be a storm in a teacup and blow over quickly.

"You're very quiet. Are you okay?" She'd almost forgotten Lynn was still on the phone.

"I'm fine. Just a bit preoccupied. These last few days have been a blur of numbers and figures. Casino books make corporate records look refreshingly dreary by comparison. I can't wait to settle back into my peacefully dull routine."

"Nothing's dull around here. Whitlow gave his resignation. It turned out Lacey wasn't the first young employee who's been under his desk. There's a class action suit in the works. It's all anyone's talking about."

"Wow." That could mean a partnership spot opening up. Not that she'd be eligible. She'd likely be considered too young. Still…

"Old goat. It's amazing what men will risk for a little nooky. Makes you glad to be a woman."

She laughed. "Hardly. The men who get themselves into trouble are usually doing something with a woman." Someone like her, for example, who would apparently risk her career for a few brief moments of bliss.

It didn't make any sense at all, yet she'd done it.

"True. Humans are irrational creatures. That's what makes us so interesting."

"Yes, indeed." She'd turned out to be far more dangerously human than she'd ever expected.

"Do you need anything?" Lynn's question took her by surprise.

"Not that I can think of. I'm sure I'll be back next week."

"And you've found nothing at all?"

She hesitated. "I'll tell you everything when I get back."

"So you did find something?" Lynn's voice was a breathy whisper.

"Don't twist my words. I'm still investigating." The last thing she needed was the office administrator sparking rumors.

"My lips are sealed."

"Good. Keep them that way and have a good weekend. I've got to go."

Constance hung up the phone, breathing a little faster than usual. She really wished she hadn't given Lynn the idea that something was up. On the other hand, it would have been weird to say she'd found nothing, then reveal in a day or two that in fact she had uncovered tax fraud. This whole situation was getting far too complicated.

And now she had to tell John. She wanted to email him

or text him, but somehow putting words in print felt wrong. They could be saved and used in some kind of legal situation. She didn't want to call him in case the phones were monitored. He might even record incoming and outgoing calls himself as some kind of protection. And she knew it was inappropriate to tell him before reporting back to the people who had hired her.

There was nothing for it but to hunt him down in person and figure out what to do from there.

When Constance arrived at the casino the next morning, John was in the lobby talking to Don. Since it was the weekend they had on more casual clothing: John wore a fitted shirt and faded jeans that hugged his powerful thighs and Don was dressed all in black like a movie mobster. She tugged her gaze away and headed for the bank of elevators. She didn't want to have to make polite conversation with a man she was about to report for tax fraud. Who knew how many years he'd been doing it? He could be in for a hefty fine or even a prison term.

She had no choice but to pass quite close to the two men, but she skirted around an electronic display that showed a list of the day's events so they couldn't see her.

"It's a good thing she's sweet on you." As she passed by, Don's words made her ears prick. "I don't like her snooping through our tax records. Make sure you wine and dine her tonight. We don't want her getting creative." Constance froze, despite knowing she was in a crowded lobby where others could see her, even if John and his uncle couldn't. Did Don know they were having an affair?

"My tax records are entirely accurate and I assume yours are, too." John's voice sounded dismissive. And why didn't he say something about her not being bribable? She was offended that he didn't defend her honor. On the other hand, maybe that would have been too much. He was being subtle.

Don laughed. Which sounded very false under the circumstances. "Don't you worry about me. She won't find anything in my taxes. And I'm the one who told you seducing her was a good idea. You should listen to me more often."

Constance's mouth dropped open and her heart hammered. She glanced at the bank of elevators, which now seemed about a mile away across the shiny marble floor. Had they planned this together? Was she a victim of a plot between them?

She blinked, hardly able to believe it.

"Don't be too smart for your own good, Don." John's voice made her jump. Wasn't he going to deny that they had planned her seduction? Her breathing became audible and she looked around, hoping no one was watching. She couldn't believe they were having this conversation right in the lobby where anyone could hear it.

John was now asking about a band due to perform that night. He'd simply changed the subject without contradicting Don? A sense of betrayal crept over her and chilled her blood. Suddenly she was glad she'd found the discrepancy in Don's taxes. John deserved the media's ugly attention and anything that came from it if he was the kind of person who'd deliberately set out to charm and cajole her into bed for his own purposes.

She lifted her chin and marched for the elevators as fast as she could, praying that no one would talk to her. She counted the seconds while she waited for an elevator to take her up to the office floor. What a disaster.

"Hey, Constance, where are you going?" John's voice boomed across the marble space. "It's Saturday."

She spun around.

"Up to the office floors. They are open on the weekends, I hope." She responded as primly as she could. How could he talk to her so casually in full view of the other employees and guests? Did he want them all to know they'd been intimate? Probably he did. Maybe he thought it was funny.

"Weren't you even going to say hello?"

"I could see you were in conference."

"In conference?" He laughed. "Don was just telling me about the new Maserati he ordered. Crazy. I told him I hope I won't get to practice using the Jaws of Life on it."

No mention of Don's thanking him for seducing her. And his own complicit silence. "Can we meet in your office?" She needed to talk to him. They'd gone too far for her to just go back home, report her findings and pretend they'd never slept together. The situation could blow up in her face if he decided to retaliate. Her hands were shaking and she hoped she wouldn't cry.

"But of course." His voice contained more than a hint of suggestion. "I'd be delighted to get you behind closed doors."

She glanced up at the security cameras. She hadn't even noticed them before. Hopefully no one ever listened to the tapes. "It's something serious."

All humor vanished from his expression. "About the returns?" And his voice was hushed.

"Let me tell you upstairs."

John closed the door behind them, and for once this did not lead to a passionate kiss. Which was good, because she would have had to slap him. "Is there something wrong?"

Her heart beat so fast she could barely think. "It's Don's return. He didn't declare any gambling winnings."

He frowned. "He certainly should have."

She swallowed. "The company records detail substantial winnings. You can see them for yourself in your own files."

"I'm sure there's some explanation."

She drew in an unsteady breath. "I'm telling you first because I promised I would." Though now she was having second thoughts about it. Did he really deserve it if he'd only flirted with her for his own protection? "But I have to tell my boss at Creighton Waterman, and I have to tell the BIA."

"Give me some time to figure out what's going on. I'll talk to Don."

"I can't. I'm paid to do a job here. I have to report what I found and I've already done something wrong by telling you first." *On top of all the other things I've done wrong in your bed.*

"He must have forgotten to report the winnings. Don has more money than he knows what to do with. I told you about the Maserati."

"There may well be a reasonable explanation, but I'm here to look for discrepancies and I found one. You admitted yourself that he gambles, and I've heard the same from other employees." She lifted her chin and defied him to argue with her.

"He makes no secret of it."

"Yet he didn't mention it on his tax return."

John drew in a long breath, swelling his broad chest. For a split second she ached to hug him, but instead she held herself stiffly at bay. He frowned. "Don's a key employee here. Something like this could really damage the casino's reputation. You know the kind of scrutiny we're under. I can't afford the bad publicity."

"If you don't want bad publicity perhaps you should be more careful about how you conduct yourself. Seducing the accountant who's sent to inspect your accounts probably isn't too smart, for a start." She braced for his response, glad she'd been bold enough to say it.

"That took me by surprise as much as you."

"Oh, really. That's not what I overheard downstairs."

He frowned. "You overheard Don? He was just kidding around."

"And you didn't contradict him."

His expression softened. "I didn't want to dignify his innuendo with a response. He really has no idea what happened between us."

She swallowed. "Good. As you can imagine I would appreciate it if you didn't discuss our indiscretions with anyone."

"Of course not. I never would." He held out his hand, but she stayed rigid.

"Everything that happened between us was a mistake and I regret it. Now I have a responsibility to report my findings to the people who hired me."

He took in a long slow breath, his expression grim. "The BIA is going to come down on us all like a ton of bricks."

"I have to do my job."

"I can see that." His jaw was set. She wondered for a tense moment if he'd attempt to flirt and cajole her out of making her report. He didn't. He watched her silently for what felt like an eternity.

She realized at last how utterly vulnerable she was. Her future, her career lay in this man's hands. He could end it, and ruin her reputation, in a single phone call if he chose.

"I understand." His words were cool, controlled. His eyes didn't plead with her, but the emotion she saw in them reminded her of the tender moments they'd shared.

At least she'd thought at the time they were tender moments.

"I'm going to call my contact now." She picked up her bag, burning with the desire to get out of here as fast as possible and never come back. He opened the door and stepped aside. Heat and tension flashed between them as she passed him.

Or maybe that was only in her imagination.

She heard the door click shut behind her after she passed through it, and her heart almost broke as she realized this would be the very last time she'd ever see John.

John pressed his body against the door, partly to stop himself from jerking it back open and striding after Constance. It was no use trying to argue with her. Her mind was made up and she was going to report what she found.

Could Don really have been stupid enough to fail to report his gambling activities?

He already knew the answer in his gut. He also knew how enthusiastically the circling media vultures would eat up the story.

And he couldn't even call Don, or a lawyer, because in doing so he'd have to reveal that Constance gave him privileged information. He wouldn't betray her confidence. She'd done him a big favor by telling him what she'd found. More so when she now suspected that he'd seduced her as a means to an end. He'd wanted to argue with her and try to convince her that his feelings for her came from the heart but there was no way she'd believe him now. She'd assume he was trying to butter her up and convince her to conceal her findings, which would only make her more suspicious and angry.

He cursed and banged his fist on the door. Why did life have to get so complicated? Everything was going smoothly until Constance Allen came along. His once-wild uncle had seemed to be settling into the life of a prosperous and trustworthy executive. Everyone in the tribe was getting along well, which was no easy feat when you brought people from all over the country to a small town in the sticks. And business was booming.

Now the harsh spotlight would fall on them once again. John knew as well as anyone that if someone was looking for a reason to make the Nissequot disappear, they could try to use this as a starting point and keep the tribe tied up in legal wrangling until the moon turned blue. That was much the same strategy that had been used by the powers that be to whittle away the tribe's land and population in the first place.

His number-one priority was to make sure that didn't happen. His second priority would be to forget all about Constance Allen. Her findings threatened to tear the fabric of the tribe. If anyone found out he'd been intimate with her while she was looking for dirt on them, it would undermine their trust in him. Don already suspected that they'd had an affair. John certainly hadn't confirmed his uncle's suspicions, but maybe by simply ignoring Don's snide comments, he'd tacitly admitted something. He'd have to manage Don carefully—never an easy feat—to make sure he didn't decide to throw hints to the press and make this ugly situation into a hot scandalous mess that could bring them all down.

He growled in frustration. Just this morning life had looked so rosy and promising. He'd missed having Constance in his bed last night due to preexisting plans with an old friend, but he'd consoled himself with the prospect of having her there for many years to come.

Not anymore. It had literally never crossed his mind that she would find something amiss. He knew the books of this casino way better than he knew the backs of his hands, and he'd vouch for them with his life. The financial affairs of the tribal members were also his concern, and he'd been pretty confident about them, too.

But Don? Apparently the smoke the media was fanning had come from a fire somewhere, and who knew what else that slippery old devil might be up to. His hand itched to pick up his phone and call his uncle, but he held the urge in check. He owed Constance that much.

But no more.

Tears blurred Constance's eyes by the time she hurried across the parking lot to her car. She climbed in and slammed the door, started the ignition with trembling fingers, and pulled out of the parking lot as fast as she could. She felt like a traitor here, which was ridiculous since she had no personal allegiance to the New Dawn casino. She shouldn't have any personal feelings for its founder, either.

The problem was that she did. Hearing that he'd discussed seducing her with his uncle should kill them stone dead. Was she a fool to believe John's denial? She wanted to believe him. And she remembered only too well how wonderful she'd felt with John's arms around her. How she'd come alive in his bed, letting herself explore a sensual and passionate side she'd never dared admit to before.

It would be very hard to just bury all those feelings again, even if the relationship had been in the wrong place, at the wrong time, with the wrong man.

She needed to call the BIA as soon as possible, just in case John did succumb to the temptation to warn his uncle. She couldn't afford to have word get out that she'd spoken to him about her findings. Nicola Moore had told her to get in touch at any time of the day or night if she had something important to report. She pulled into the parking lot of a fast-food restaurant and dialed Nicola Moore's cell number.

When Nicola answered, Constance got right to the point. "I'm sorry to call you on the weekend, but I've found a discrepancy." She kept her voice as calm as she could. "It might be nothing—" she swallowed "—but I've done all the research I can reasonably do into the situation from my end."

She told Moore about Don's reported gambling and its absence from his tax return. She'd only looked at one year, but she knew that this probably wasn't an isolated issue. From here on out it would be a matter for the IRS to investigate further. Her work was done, and she should feel a sense of pride and accomplishment in it, yet somehow she felt just the opposite.

"Good work. This will give us a foothold for further investigation."

"I didn't find any irregularities in the financials for the casino itself, just for this one executive." She wanted to limit the damage she'd cause to the New Dawn's reputation. Not that it should be any of her business.

"We've had our eye on Don Fairweather for some time. It's hard to understand why John Fairweather lets him play a substantial role in the company when he has a shady past."

"He's not directly involved in the financial operations at all. He books the bands and handles PR." Constance heard herself speaking quickly, defending John's choice to employ his uncle, and cursed herself for standing up for him. Obviously, she still cared about him. She'd let herself believe that he had real feelings for her, and now she felt foolish for being so gullible. She couldn't get away fast enough. She knew that John felt strongly about including all members of the family—and by extension the Nissequot tribe—and managing them appropriately. She also knew he couldn't control their personal choices.

"So I'm done here, right? It would be really awkward for me to hang around after making these accusations." She realized that didn't sound professional. In reality it had been awkward all along to have people know she was there looking for trouble. But she truly couldn't stand it if she had to see John again now that she knew the truth about his involvement with her.

"Yes, we'll have our legal team take it from here. Just forward all the relevant paperwork to me and I'll be in touch if I need anything further. Good work."

Heart heavy, Constance gathered her belongings from her hotel room and immediately began the long, lonely drive back to Ohio. Back to her former life of quiet work in her gray office and quiet evenings at home with her parents.

No kisses waited for her. No strong arms. No fiery passion to bring her body to life.

The worst part was that somehow her mind—or her body—couldn't accept that it was all over. She kept waiting for the phone to ring. For John to say that he'd known all along she was there for a reason, that it didn't make any difference that she'd done her job, even if it meant his family member would get in trouble.

Part of her still believed that what they'd shared was real. They'd had such great conversations, and experienced so much intimacy. Surely even if he'd started out to soften her up for business reasons, it had developed into something more. Or was it all in her head?

They hadn't even said goodbye. The last thing he'd said to her was, "I understand." But did he?

Would he have preferred for her to lie to her boss? To lie to the BIA? Then his little plan would have really paid off. She would have proved that she'd really loved him. Lucky thing she was not the kind of person who would ever do that. If she had nothing else left, at least she had her integrity, and of that she was fiercely proud.

At the office that Monday, her boss, Lucinda Waldron, was all smiles. "Well done, Constance. This was a tough assignment and once again you've proven yourself to be one of our rising stars. And it's a real bonus that you don't have a family to worry about. It's hard to find an employee who doesn't mind spending some time away from home. I have an interesting assignment coming up in Omaha that I think you'd be perfect for. I should know more details in a day or two."

"Great." She managed a smile. Omaha? And why not? As her boss pointed out, she had no life and no obligations. Not even a pet to worry about. They could ship her all over the country to ferret through companies' books and no one would even care except her parents, who would have to do their own dishes after dinner.

In her office she looked through her in-box with a heavy heart. All the employee expense reports for the last three months were in there. She was chosen to go through them, as she was considered the most trustworthy and least indulgent employee. Lynn had told her that just the idea that Constance Allen would be checking their expenses kept people from putting frivolous items on there.

Great.

"I've found the perfect man for you." Lynn peeped around her door.

"Shh! Someone will hear you." She didn't want to chat about men and dating. The whole thing seemed like a really bad idea. Obviously her judgment was questionable at best and who knew what might happen if she started putting herself in the way of available men so soon after John.

"It's not a crime to date, you know. Do you remember Lance from corporate?"

"I'd never date a coworker." And mostly she remembered Lance's receding chin. Which wasn't fair, really, as he had always been perfectly nice to her.

"You won't have to. He offered his resignation. He's going to KPMG."

"Which likely means he'll be moving to a different city. Long distance would never work."

"Why not? Better than not dating at all. Besides, you could always move."

"Leave Cleveland? What would my parents do?"

"I'm sure they'd survive."

"I'm not attracted to him."

"You barely know him. You have to give someone a chance. You might have amazing chemistry."

She looked right at Lynn. "Are you attracted to him?"

Lynn bit her lip and thought for a moment. "No. But I figured you'd want someone stable and quiet and…"

"Boring? What if I want someone wild and dangerous and exciting?" She leaned back in her chair. "What if I want someone totally different from me, who can help shake me out of my dull and rigid existence and make me look at the world with fresh eyes?"

Lynn stared at her. "Do you?"

She adjusted her glasses. "I don't want to date anyone." There was no way she could even consider looking at another man while John's handsome face hovered in her consciousness. And while his betrayal echoed in her heart. She still could hardly believe their whole affair had been planned from the start. "I have too many other things going on."

"Like reorganizing your bookshelf?"

"There's a church fund-raiser to plan."

"There's always a church fund-raiser to plan. I'm not going to let you waste your life anymore. It's time you burst out of your shell." Lynn winked and walked away.

Constance sank back in her chair. If only Lynn knew that she'd already left her shell and would never be happy in it again.

Ten

John walked into Don's rather lavish office and threw the newspapers down on his desk. "See what you've done?" Stories about the tax evasion had leaked to the press—or been planted.

"It's a load of bull."

"So you didn't gamble and win that money?" He crossed his arms and waited for a response.

"I don't remember."

"That won't cut it."

"It's worked for some American presidents I could name."

"Well, you aren't one, and you aren't senile either, so you'd better hire a lawyer and figure out what the two of you are going to say. The New Dawn is not going under the bus with you, Don. You know how I feel about following the rules. We're under way more scrutiny than the average business and I don't condone any activity that could even be seen as bending the rules."

"Sometimes you need to redefine a rule."

"Now is not one of those times. Since you aren't denying that you've gambled and failed to declare it, I have no choice but to terminate your position."

Don rose to his feet, frowning. "Are you kicking me out of the tribe, too?"

"This is business, Don, purely business. You'll always be family, but I can't have you working at the New Dawn while you're under investigation for breaking the law."

"Is it a paid leave of absence?"

John clenched his hand into a fist. "Is this my hand or is it a deadly weapon?"

"All right, all right. I can't believe you're just kicking me out. Whatever happened to innocent until proven guilty?"

"If you were declaring your innocence, I might feel differently, but you're not. I trusted you, Don. You've been my confidant and right-hand man at almost every phase of this project. I can't believe you'd risk it all to save yourself a few pennies you can well afford to part with."

"I'll pay whatever I owe."

"You know it won't be as easy as that. They're going to dig into your papers going back years."

His uncle's face darkened. "That won't be good. I told you I didn't want you to give her my returns."

"You didn't tell me it's because they were fraudulent."

"I didn't write any lies on them. I may have just not told the whole truth."

John suppressed a curse. "All this could have been easily avoided if you just did what you were supposed to do." Despite his anger, John felt a twinge of sorrow for Don. Why were some people constitutionally unable to play by the rules? "If you think a law is wrong then you can work to change it. You can't just ignore it."

Don shoved some items from his drawer—expensive Cross pens, technological gadgets—into his leather briefcase. "Everything's easy for you. You've always been the golden boy."

"I've worked my ass off for everything I've achieved and I'm not going to let you throw it all away." John wanted to take Don by the scruff of the neck and hurl him down the hallway, but he restrained himself. He also wanted to cuss his uncle out for ruining all his elaborate plans to keep Constance in his life, but he knew better than to clue Don in to that secret.

Don looked up from his desk and peered at him. "Shame you didn't use your charm to run Constance Allen off the property as I suggested."

"Charm usually has the opposite effect."

"Not on a sexless automaton like that one. A calculator in a suit."

John's hands were forming fists again without his permission. "You keep your thoughts on Ms. Allen to yourself."

"Oh, did I touch a nerve? I suppose you've seen more of what's under that suit than I gave you credit for. What if I tell the press about that, huh?"

"You wouldn't."

"Wouldn't I?"

"There's nothing to tell," he growled. "Just get out of here before I throw you out." Fury churned in his gut. Now that Constance had overturned Don's applecart, there was basically no way he could invite her into the family without it causing a major rift. Not that she'd want to come, anyway. He'd promised her all would be aboveboard, only to be proved wrong by his own flesh and blood. And now she thought he'd seduced her in a deliberate ploy to interfere with her investigation.

"I can see you have feelings for her." Don hoisted his bag onto his shoulder.

"I don't. Except that I'm mad she wouldn't let me deal with this myself. I could have made you declare all your back taxes without dragging the law into this."

A knock on the door made them both turn. "Mr. Fairweather." Angie, one of the desk clerks, appeared. "The police are here."

"I knew they'd turn up sooner or later." John shoved a hand through his hair. "Why not just send them up?"

"I'm so glad you're back home, dear." Constance peeled carrots while her mom chopped chicken breast for a pie. She'd been home for three days and they'd all settled back into their dull, familiar routine as if she'd never left. "Maybe you can talk some sense into your father about eating better. His cholesterol still isn't down where it should be and he keeps insisting on eggs and sausage for breakfast in the morning. He's even making it himself when I refuse."

"I'll bake some healthy muffins tomorrow morning. I think the best strategy is to tempt him away from the bad things he loves rather than just making him eat stuff he hates."

"You're so right, dear. I hadn't really thought of that. I've been trying to convince him to eat oatmeal and he won't even touch it. I knew you'd come up with something. I hope your job isn't going to send you away again."

"Actually my boss was talking about an assignment in Omaha. They seem to like the fact that I'm single and have no obligations."

"But you have an obligation to me and your father. You should tell them that."

"You should get used to me being gone, Mom. What if I get married?"

Her mom laughed. "You? You're married to your job. I can't even imagine you with a man. And honestly, sometimes I think they're more trouble than they're worth."

Constance's grip tightened on the peeler. Did her own mother seriously not think that she'd want to get married and have a family? Then again, why should she? Constance hadn't dated anyone at all the entire time she'd been living at home and she'd rebuffed several efforts to set her up with people she had no interest in or attraction to.

The truth was, she hadn't been interested in anyone until she met John. Why did she have to finally fall for someone so unsuitable and impossible? It could never have worked out, even if their affair hadn't been a shocking breach of professional conduct. He was a seasoned playboy who had apparently seduced her for his own purposes—at least initially—and if they hadn't been torn apart by circumstance he would have grown bored with her and cast her aside eventually.

"Why are your hands shaking?" Constance saw her mom's penetrating gray gaze fall on her fingers and she tried to peel faster. "I knew you never should have gone to that den of vice. You've looked like a ghost ever since you got back. Sally told me she read on the internet there's a big investigation going on there now. Tax evasion. I told her it was you that found out about it." She clucked her tongue. "Hardly a surprise, of course. It's always the people with the most money who are least willing to part with it. Still, I'm sure it was exhausting having to interact with people like that."

"I'm just tired." No need to mention all the stray emotion racking her and keeping her awake at night. "It was a challenging job. A lot of papers and computer files to go through. I worked really long hours." *And then played even longer hours.*

The memory of John's strong arms around her haunted her in the dead of night. Her body still tingled with awareness whenever she thought of him. Which was unfair, because she knew that right now he must hate her.

She'd seen the stories online. Don had been arrested

and charged with tax evasion and John had bailed him out with five hundred thousand dollars of his own money. He certainly wouldn't be lying around in bed thinking about how much he missed the woman who'd given the IRS probable cause for a full investigation of New Dawn. There was even talk of the casino being closed down while it was under investigation, and she knew from her examination of the books that would mean millions in losses for John and the tribe.

When he thought of her it must be with resentment and anger. Still, if she had to do it over, she wouldn't do anything differently. She'd bent her rules by leaking the information about John's uncle to him, but in the end, she'd stuck to her principles and done the job she was paid to do.

The affair with John was a whole different story. Would she let that happen again? She wasn't entirely sure she'd let it happen in the first place. It had just happened. What evolved between them had crept over her like a thunderstorm and she suspected there was nothing she could have done to control or stop the thunder and lightning flashing in her body—and her heart—when John was around.

Lucky thing she wouldn't see him again. The IRS had taken over the investigation and her firm had sent their final bill to the BIA. She could wash her hands of the whole sticky mess.

Except that she couldn't get John Fairweather out of her mind.

She'd just scraped the carrot peelings into the bin and was removing the full bag when the door to the kitchen flung open and her dad peered in. "Son of a gun, Constance, you're not going to believe what that fellow on the news just said."

"What, Dad?" Probably something to do with the upcoming local election he was up in arms about.

"That Native American from the casino who was arrested for tax evasion just claimed that the leader of the tribe engaged in personal relations with the accountant who came to investigate them. Isn't that you?"

Constance fumbled and the bin liner and its contents spilled onto the floor. "What?" Her voice was a shaky whisper. Blood roared in her ears. Or maybe it was the sound of her whole world crashing down around her.

"Said he wasn't the only one bending a few rules and he thought people should know the truth about the BIA's investigator who pointed the finger at him." Her dad's voice trailed off as he surveyed the mess on the floor. "It's not true, is it, sweet?"

She scrambled to pick up the slimy carrot peelings, plastic cheese wrappers and crumpled damp paper towels from the tile floor and shove them back in the bag. Could she really lie to her own parents?

"Constance Allen." Her mother's voice rang out. "You heard your father. Tell us this minute that these evil accusations are entirely false."

She rose shakily to her feet and held her hands under the tap, trying to rinse off the garbage. "They're not false." She couldn't even look at them as she said it. She picked up the sponge and knelt back down to try to wipe up the mess.

"You had an affair with the man you were sent to dig up dirt on?" Her mother moved closer.

"I was sent to look at the company's books. I did my job." She rinsed the sponge and wrung it out. Then she looked up at her parents standing there, so close to her, in the small kitchen where she'd made dinner with her mother for so many years. "I didn't mean to do anything else, but..." How did she explain what happened? "He was very handsome and kind, and I was very foolish."

"I have no doubt that man deliberately set out to seduce

you in order to pervert the course of your investigation." Her mother's mouth pinched into a tight knot.

"Maybe he did." She put the sponge down, hands still trembling. "But I never altered anything about the way I conducted my work. As you've already heard, I uncovered tax evasion by one of his relatives."

"Did you sleep with this man?" Her mother's hissed question made her shrink inside her clothes.

"Sarah! How can you ask such a question?" Her dad's shocked expression only deepened Constance's sense of humiliation and sadness.

"I did, Mom. I'm sorry, Dad. It's just the truth. I'm not proud of it. To this day I really don't know what came over me. He was quite a man." She let out a sigh and wished she could release the tension that heated the air in the kitchen almost to the boiling point. "Apparently I'm only human after all."

"I knew you should never have gone to that gambling establishment. A place like that isn't safe for a nice young girl."

"It's not the place, Mom. It's me. I've been living under a rock too long. I didn't realize how lonely I was. How much intimacy and affection could appeal to me."

"This man must have no sense of honor at all if he'd tell the media about your...interaction with him." Her father's usually placid brow had furrowed. "Then again, it was the other man on the news. The one you accused of tax evasion." He cleared his throat. "I suppose the dust will settle sooner or later."

"Oh, dear." Her mother's hand was now pressed to her mouth. "You'll be fired, won't you?"

"Probably." Her voice was hollow. She had no appetite whatsoever for carrots and chicken potpie. "In fact, I suppose I should offer my resignation."

"There's always a spot for you behind our counter. Our customers do love you," her dad tried to reassure her.

Constance cringed at the thought of serving people who'd heard about her transgressions.

"Are you trying to set our daughter up as a carnival sideshow, Brian? She can't be seen in public with scandal like this flying around. Though I suppose she could reorganize the shelves in the stockroom. Goodness, what will the pastor think?"

Constance hit breaking point and watched herself throw the sponge down in the sink and run from the room, leaving them staring after her. She'd known it was wrong to sleep with John and she'd done it anyway. He had been too much for her to resist. Now she'd lose her career over him and she probably deserved it. At least stupidity wasn't a crime and she wouldn't end up with a criminal record for her mistake.

She hurled herself down on the bed, tears hovering just behind her eyes. How was John coping with all of this? Was he embarrassed by the news of their liaison becoming public, or did he think it was funny? She'd loved the way that nothing rattled him and he went about his business with such good humor.

Maybe she could learn to do the same. She'd need all the sense of humor she could muster to get through the coming days and weeks.

John pounded along the trail, past the grazing cows and towards the shady woods. It wasn't his style to run away from problems, but right now he needed to let off steam. A twig snapped behind him and he spun around, expecting to see another nosy reporter.

Worse, he saw Don, sweating and panting, trying to catch up with him.

"Get lost."

"Wait! I want to apologize."

"It's way, way too late for that." Anger rushed him—again—and he turned and kept running, faster. At least his uncle Don was one problem he really could outrun.

But the footsteps got closer. "You forgot I was a sprinter in high school," rasped Don.

"Sprinting will only get you but so far. Like cheating, and lying." John kept running, though the urge to turn around and knock Don to the ground tightened his biceps.

"I promise I'll never lie or cheat again." Don gasped the words as he ran. "I'll never gamble again."

"How about if you never speak again?" John yelled. Don kept getting closer, his wiry frame must be fitter than it looked.

"That I can't promise. See? I'm not lying." Don was almost level with him.

John spun around and shoved out his hand, which caught Don in the chest with the satisfying force of a punch. Don doubled over as the air rushed out of his lungs. "I should knock you senseless."

"But that would be a crime and you're well above that."

"Exactly." John looked down on Don, who panted, hands on his knees. "And I'm trying to build the Nissequot tribe, not kill off its members with my bare hands."

"I really am sorry."

"For what? There's so much for you to regret that I can't keep track. You're being investigated for fraud along with the business I've staked everything on. You could go to prison. And on top of that you decided to announce to the local news that I had an affair with the BIA's investigator."

"I was mad at you. I didn't think they they'd really believe me. I didn't even believe it myself. You should have told me it was true and I would have kept my mouth shut. It is true, isn't it?"

"As if I would ever confide in you. I wouldn't trust

you with my grocery list at this point." He should have rebuffed Don's innuendo, instead of ignoring it. Denied his suspicions.

Except that they were true.

Even now he couldn't get Constance out of his mind for a solid minute. He'd hoped that the vision of her soft hazel eyes would fade. It had been three days and now he was seeing her face everywhere he looked.

"I know you think I'm stupid, and in all honesty, sometimes I am," Don panted, sweat dripping from his tanned forehead. His black T-shirt was soaked through. "But I know there was something between you and Miss Constance Allen. And not just sex, either. If you ask me, you're going to pieces without her."

John jerked to his feet. "Going to pieces? You're the one losing your mind. I've never been calmer. I'm just trying to think of how to prevent the enterprise we spent years building, and the tribe we've poured our lifeblood into, from being destroyed by a few strokes of a pen. I'm not even thinking about...her."

Don rose to his feet and wiped sweat from his brow. "You can't fool me, boy. I've known you too long. You need to go after her and win her back."

He certainly wasn't going to tell Don that he'd been thinking about it. "I'm sure the media would just love that."

"I'm serious. It's not a crime to fall in love. She still did her job and ratted me out."

"She has principles, unlike a certain scumbag relative of mine."

Don crossed his arms. "I'm serious. I don't want you blaming me for you losing the love of your life as well as creating an embarrassing mess in the press."

John blew out hard. "I don't need your advice to run my life, thanks. I think I can do a much better job of that by myself."

Don persisted. "So go get her."

John drew in a breath. The breeze cooled his face and a bird chirped in a nearby tree. "Although right now I hate you more than any man alive, for once you might be right about something."

John ordered a ring from Tiffany's in Manhattan and arranged to have it couriered to meet him at the airport in Cleveland. He chose a simple ring, since he knew Constance wouldn't like anything ostentatious. He had to guess the size, but they assured him it would be easy to fix if necessary. He chartered a plane at the local airport and boarded it with anticipation snapping through his muscles.

Was he jumping the gun by planning a proposal rather than simply inviting her back into his life? Possibly. But getting her to move from Ohio to Massachusetts would take a huge leap of faith on her part and he wanted her to know that he meant to offer her everything—including marriage.

The word echoed in his brain. Marriage was permanent. For life. Usually that would scare him right out the door, but now it had a reassuring, solid ring to it that steadied his hand on the wheel. His grandmother always said that when you met the right person, you just knew. You didn't have to date the woman for years or know every single thing about her to know that you were meant for each other. And his grandparents had been together long enough to test his grandmother's theory.

John trusted his gut. It had steered him right many times in the past, even when everyone else and basic common sense suggested otherwise. His gut told him that Constance was the woman he'd been waiting for all these years. He needed her in his life, in his arms, in his bed.

Now all he had to do was convince her. And that meant

convincing her that his intentions had been honorable from the start of their affair.

He arrived at the Cleveland airport and met the courier with the ring in the arrivals terminal. The diamond solitaire was as simple and lovely as he'd hoped, and his nerves sizzled as he tucked it into his pants pocket. Then he rented a car and programmed the GPS to take him to the address he'd found on the internet.

Blood thundered in his veins as he pulled into the driveway of her parents' modest house in a sleepy Cleveland neighborhood. She'd probably be freaked out that he'd stalked her online to find her address. If she wasn't sufficiently alarmed just to see him here at all. Her car was already in the driveway, so she was here. And the large white van with a hardware store decal on the side must belong to her parents, who were probably home, too. He parked behind it.

He never got nervous going into all-or-nothing business meetings or negotiating million-dollar deals. Climbing the Allen family's scuffed doorstep, however, he felt his nerves tingling. He pushed the bell and heard a chime sound on the other side of the door.

"Oh, goodness. Who can that be?" He could hear a woman's stressed-sounding voice in the distance and could make out a person's fast-approaching silhouette through the patterned glass oval in the door. He steadied himself as the door swung open and plastered on an encouraging smile. A small woman with a neat brown bob appeared in the doorway.

"Hello, you must be Mrs. Allen." He extended his hand.

"Leave us alone," the woman said, and then slammed the door in his face. Maybe she thought he was a reporter.

He rang the doorbell again. "I'm not a journalist," he called. "Or a salesman." He saw her blurry silhouette halt. "I'm a friend of Constance's."

He watched the woman turn and walk back through the glass. The door cracked open and a pair of very suspicious gray eyes peered at him. "Constance has been taken ill."

"What?" He stepped forward, one hand on the door. "What's wrong with her?"

"Who are you?" Constance's mom was a little shorter than her daughter, and dressed in a plaid blouse and navy slacks.

"My name is John Fairweather." He extended his hand again. "I'm pleased to meet you." He quietly put one knee in front of the door in case she tried to slam it again. Not a moment too soon, because he soon felt the force of the door against his arm and leg.

"Get out of my doorway, you…you scum!"

John drew in a deep breath. "I think there's a misunderstanding. Constance investigated my company, but it was my uncle's records that she found wanting, not mine."

The small woman stopped pushing on the door and came alarmingly close, her face crinkling with rage. "You seduced an innocent young girl," she hissed. "You should be ashamed of yourself."

He decided not to protest that Constance wasn't that young or that innocent. "Your daughter is a very unique and special person, and I'm sure that much of the credit for that goes to you, Mrs. Allen. I admire her integrity and am proud to know her."

"Well, she doesn't want anything to do with you, that's for sure. She'll probably get fired now that ugly rumors are flying around." At least she wasn't trying to slam the door on him anymore. "What have you got to say for yourself about that?"

"Constance has nothing to hide. She did her job with thoroughness and even ruthlessness. I'm sure her employer will find no fault with her. May I see her, please?"

Was she really sick? She must be under a lot of stress.

As John mulled it over, a timid-looking man with a receding hairline appeared at the end of the hallway. "What's going on, dear?"

"This is John Fairweather, Brian." She spoke very deliberately, without taking her eyes off him. John watched her husband put two and two together.

"You're not welcome here, I'm afraid." He glanced nervously at his wife. "You'd best go back to where you came from."

"I'm in love with your daughter." Desperation made him cut right to the point. He knew Constance must be in there somewhere. "Please, let me see her."

He smiled, to hopefully seem less threatening, but he was serious about what he said next. "I'm not going to leave until I talk to her. I'll camp out on your front lawn if necessary." Since their front lawn was about as big as a king-size bed and had a fake fountain on it, he hoped it wouldn't come to that.

Mrs. Allen glanced up and down the street. The sun was setting and so far the only people watching them were two kids on bikes. She narrowed her eyes and shot him a chilling look. "Perhaps you'd better come in."

He tried not to beam with too much excitement as he stepped over the threshold into their narrow hallway.

"Constance, dear," her father called up the stairs. "Could you come down, sweetheart?"

All eyes turned anxiously to the gloomy stairs. But no door opened. Listening hard, John could hear music playing up there. Impatience and excitement fired through him. "I think she's got the radio on and can't hear you. Would it be okay with you if I go knock on her door?"

Normally he'd have marched straight up, but since he intended for these people to be his future mother- and father-in-law, more delicate handling was called for.

The Allens looked at each other. Sarah had closed the

door behind John to block out the prying eyes of neighbors. "I suppose so," she muttered. "You can hardly make things worse than they already are."

He bounded up the stairs, feeling his pants pocket on the way to check the ring was still there, and knocked on the door. A song by Adele was playing.

"I need some time alone, Mom."

"It's me. John."

The music snapped off.

"What?"

The sweet sound of her voice made his heart swell, and his fingers reached for the door handle. But he hesitated. What if she wasn't decent? He didn't want to blow it.

"John Fairweather. I drove here to see you."

The door flung open so fast he felt his hair shift in the breeze. She was dressed in striped pajama pants and a white T-shirt and looked as though she'd been crying. She also looked unbearably beautiful and fragile, and he wanted to take her in his arms.

"You've got quite a nerve." She said it softly, as if she wasn't really listening to herself. She studied his face, then he felt her take in the rest of his body before looking back into his eyes with a confused expression.

"That's hardly news." He felt a grin spreading across his face. "I missed you."

"Did you tell Don about our affair?" Her gaze hardened. Pain hovered in her eyes.

"Never. He made it all up, in fact. I never told him anything about us. He was just mad—mostly at me because I fired him from his position."

"But you didn't deny it."

"I can't deny it. It's the truth." A smile tugged at the corner of his mouth, but he struggled to suppress it.

She frowned. "It's a shame you didn't get what you wanted, isn't it?"

"What do you mean?"

"It's a pity your plot to seduce me didn't throw me off the course and make me leave. Or convince me to cover up the truth. I overheard your conversation with Don in the lobby."

"There was never any kind of plot. Don suggested it, but I never had the slightest intention of following through."

"You just kissed me on the first night you met me because I'm so unbelievably irresistible?" She cocked her head.

"Exactly." The smile struggled over his mouth again.

"I'm not that dumb, John."

"You're not dumb at all. You're sharp as a tack and that's one of the many reasons I'm crazy about you."

She frowned and looked confused. "Why are you here? I'm not going to deny the affair if that's what you're hoping. I'd rather lose my career than tell a lie that big."

"I feel the same way." He reached for the ring in his pocket. No use beating about the bush. When she saw it she'd know he was serious. "I realize we've only known each other a short time." He pulled out the box and watched her brow furrow. "But there's something between us, something different." For once, he struggled for words. "I love you, Constance. I love you and I need you in my life. I've never met anyone like you before and I want to spend the rest of my days with you. Will you marry me?"

Eleven

Constance stared at John. It was hard enough to comprehend that he was here in her bedroom. She certainly didn't believe that he'd just asked her to marry him.

"Aren't you mad at me?" She'd pictured him cursing her and wishing she'd never been born. She knew the kind of scrutiny his casino and his whole tribe were under right now.

"For being honest and trustworthy? No way. I love you all the more for it."

She blinked. He looked ridiculously handsome, with that wary expression on his face and the pale blue box open in his hand. And that sure was a beautiful ring.

"You can't be serious. About marrying me, I mean."

"Constance, you know me well enough to know that I wouldn't joke about something like this. I love you, and I want you to be my wife." Humor twinkled in his eyes, as usual. He was always so confident. He was sure she'd say yes.

Constance stared from his face to the ring and back. This was beyond anything she could imagine. She'd never thought for a minute that John would want to turn their affair into something permanent. She hadn't allowed herself a dream that crazy. "You can't be serious."

"Are you okay in there, Constance?" She heard her father's voice on the other side of the door, which John had closed behind him.

"Yes, Dad. I'm fine." *At least I think I am. I'm not sure. I might be dreaming.*

"You're killing me, Constance. I'm in love with you." John sank to one knee on the pale green carpet. "Please say you'll marry me."

Tears sprang to her eyes. She could hear the sincerity in his voice, feel it in the air between them. "Yes." The word sounded so strange coming from her mouth. The whole situation was so surreal. But it was the only answer she could give.

He rose to his feet, dark eyes shining. "May I kiss you?"

She bit her lip, and glanced at the door. Both of her parents were probably standing outside. She looked back at John and his loving gaze melted her. "Okay."

His lips covered hers and she lost herself in the kiss, holding him tight. Kissing him again was such a sweet relief after the lonely nights and anxious days since she'd left him. He wrapped his strong arms around her, holding her up as her already shaky knees threatened to give way.

"God, I missed you so much," he breathed, pressing her against him when they finally broke for air. "I hate being without you. Will you come back with me right now?"

She bit her lip. "What about my job? They're being really supportive. They don't believe the allegations that I had an affair with you and I couldn't bring myself to admit it. Now they'll have good cause to fire me when they find out it's true and I didn't confess."

He ran his thumb over her lip as his face creased into a grin. "I do like the way you take your responsibilities so seriously. It's one of the many sexy things about you. They're going to know for sure that we had an affair when you tell them you're marrying me."

"Yes, but I need to reassure them that it didn't interfere with me fulfilling my professional responsibilities. What if they think you're back here to curry favor in the hope that I can get the IRS off your back?" She was only half kidding.

"I don't live my life worrying about what other people think." Undeterred, he kissed her mouth softly. "I know that if I choose to do what's right, I can hold my head high in front of anyone. Including your parents." He glanced in the direction of the door with a wink. "Do you think we should go tell them?"

She nodded, apprehension zinging inside her. "I suppose there's no way around that."

He opened the door to find both of them standing in the hallway outside her bedroom.

"We overheard," said her mother, with a dazed expression.

"Mom!"

"And we appreciate this young man having the honor and decency to make an honest woman of you." Her mother looked right at John.

"You do?" John looked astonished.

Her father cleared his throat. "Under the circumstances I'm truly convinced that you love our daughter. I won't say we approve of the business you're in, but we have no intention but to wish you both the best."

"You do?" It was Constance's turn to express her shock and disbelief. "I'll have to move to Massachusetts." She figured she might as well lay it all out.

"And we hope that you'll both move to Massachusetts with us," John cut in. "You'll find it's a lovely place to live."

"We do have a business to run here," Sarah explained. "But I'm sure we'd be happy to come visit."

Constance stared from one of her parents to the other,

then back to John. Did he have magical powers of persuasion? The media had as much as accused him of that when he'd created a tribe out of a few family members and a multimillion-dollar company on a few weedy acres in the backwoods.

"I look forward to getting to know you both." John shook their hands heartily. "Will you allow me to take you all out to dinner to celebrate?"

Her father still looked a bit stunned, but in a happy way. "We'd be delighted."

After a congenial dinner at her parents' favorite Italian restaurant, John and Constance drove to a nearby hotel. Once inside the room, with the door closed, they stopped and stared at each other. "Am I dreaming?" She stood about one foot from him, beside the bed, in the dimly lit room. "Because I have had strange and vivid dreams lately."

"If you're dreaming then I guess it means I'm in your dream." He held her gaze. "Which is fine with me. As long as neither of us wakes up." His lips curved into a mischievous half smile.

She felt her own now-familiar smile creep to her mouth in response. "I don't think either of us is the type to sleepwalk through life, so I suspect we're wide awake right now."

He lifted a brow. "I think you'll have to pinch me to find out."

She inhaled slowly, then reached around for his backside. It wasn't easy to pinch that much hard muscle, but she managed, at the cost of heating her blood a few more degrees.

"Yep. I'm awake." His eyes had darkened with desire. "Now for you." He slid his hands around her hips until he was cupping her rear. Then he squeezed and lifted her up so fast that she gasped as adrenaline rushed through her. "Uh-huh. You are, too." Still holding her off the ground, he let her rest against his big body and slowly slide down. She felt the hard jut of his erection through his dark pants, and it made her breath catch. "Awake, and if I'm not mistaken, every bit as aroused as I am."

She bit her lip and nodded. Heat pooled deep inside her and clouded her thinking. When her toes touched the floor, her fingers reached for the buttons on his shirt. She could hear her breathing quicken as she pulled each button from its hole and exposed his broad, muscled chest. His big fingers struggled with the tiny buttons on her blouse, and his expression of intense concentration made her chuckle.

She kissed his chest and inhaled the rich, masculine scent of him, then let her mouth trail down to where his pants sat low on his hips. It excited her to see how aroused he was. She heard his breath hitch and saw his stomach contract as she kissed his hard flesh through the expensive fabric of his pants. Then she undid the catch and the zipper with trembling fingers and slid the pants down over his powerful thighs.

It drove her crazy that this man was so intensely excited by her, ordinary little Constance Allen, who spent her days surrounded by file cabinets and calculators. But his passion-filled gaze and fierce erection left no doubt.

He slid her skirt and stockings off and pulled her onto the bed. For a moment they lay side by side, enjoying the vision of each other naked.

Seeing their surroundings made her remember that they were in a busy hotel with paper-thin walls and middle managers making phone calls in the rooms around them. "Maybe we should put the radio on."

He winked. "You're so practical. I love that about you.

And you're right. We don't need everyone in the Inn and Suites to hear your cries of passion." He reached for the radio next to the bed and turned the dial until he found a slow song. "And speaking of practical, I still have enough sense left to remember to use a condom." He fished in his bag and pulled out the packet, then opened it and settled back on the bed with her.

The soft sounds of sexy music filled the room as he rested his broad hand on her hip and slid it slowly up her waist to her breast. She watched his chest rise as he ran his fingers over her breast, stimulating her nipple. She was already so aroused that she let out a gasp. "I want you inside me," she pleaded, hardly able to believe it was her talking. She'd had no idea until she met John that she was capable of this kind of desire.

"With no foreplay?" He looked surprised.

"I don't need foreplay right now." She pressed her mouth to his for one breathless instant. "And I can see you don't either."

"True." He groaned as she wrapped her hand around him, then took the condom from him and rolled it on. With confidence and conviction that surprised her, she slid underneath him and guided him inside her. Her hips rose as he entered her and the sense of relief and exhilaration took her breath away. It felt so right. She lifted her hips to meet his and they moved together, both already on the brink of explosion, so much pent-up need and desire ready to burst over them.

"I love you." Her confession sprang from her lips—she couldn't hold back the words. Her feelings for him had been growing inside her from the first moment they kissed—maybe even the first moment they met—and she could now acknowledge what they meant. As she came to this realization, she felt the first waves of her orgasm spread through her like a tornado unwinding.

"I love you, too, sweetheart." He moved over her with a slow intensity that unraveled her completely. "I love you so, so…" His words were lost as he climaxed and she gripped him as hard as she could, fingers pressing into the hard muscle of his back.

She felt him pulsing inside her, and her heart filled until she thought it would burst. She didn't care if everyone at work knew she'd had an affair with the man she was sent to investigate. She didn't care if they fired her from her job. She didn't care if she never worked in accounting again. She didn't care about anything except being here, with John, right now.

And for the rest of her life.

His big body rested so comfortably on hers. "…So much."

She wanted to laugh, but couldn't find the energy. All the anxiety and worry and tension of the last few days had been wrung out of her by their lovemaking. The aftershocks of her orgasm trickled through her, sending a silly giggle to her chest. "What have you done to me? I feel like a completely different person when I'm with you."

"With me you're exactly the person you're supposed to be. Me, too. I was so caught up in trying to make money and avoid any romantic entanglements that I was running every minute. You were so caught up in trying to be Little Miss Perfect that you needed someone to trip you right up and stop you in your tracks."

"And catch me as I fell."

She felt his chuckle vibrate through both of them. Then he rolled gently off her until they were side by side, hugging each other. "To catch you and hold you tight so you couldn't slip away." His soft kiss sent yet another smile spreading across her lips.

She remembered the ring on her finger and pulled her hand up to stare at it. One stunning diamond in a minimalist platinum setting.

"I wanted something classic and perfect, with no unnecessary embellishment. Like you."

"It's so gorgeous. It must have cost a fortune." The diamond itself was set so that it didn't stick out or look ostentatious, but on close inspection she could see it was very large.

"What's the point of having a fortune if you can't spend it on the really important things? And you're the most important thing that has ever happened to me." His voice had a raw, honest edge to it that made tears spring to her eyes.

"I feel like I should give you something, too." What did you give the man who had everything? And if he didn't have it yet, he could buy it tomorrow.

"You are. You." He pulled her fingers gently to his lips and kissed them.

The truth of his words shocked her little. In agreeing to marry him she had given herself to him, which, she knew, meant giving up her life in Ohio and moving to Massachusetts, away from all her friends and family. She'd have to quit her job even if they didn't fire her.

"What's the matter?" He stroked her cheek.

"I'm thinking about all the changes ahead. Where will I work?"

"Well, the New Dawn has been accused of nepotism, and with good reason." He winked. "We do like to employ family members."

She frowned. "What would I do there?"

He pulled back and looked at her with a serious expression. "Whatever you think is important and interesting.

Your financial expertise could certainly be put to good use. You could even take over that part of the daily operations from me so I can focus on booking celebrities and hustling some good PR. I suspect I'll be better at that than Uncle Don was."

She inhaled sharply. "I still can't believe that he went to the press about us."

"He can be a real ass sometimes. Especially since he didn't even know we actually were involved." He ran his thumb over her lips. "I'm providing him with the best legal counsel so hopefully he won't spend the next few decades in jail, but he might wish he was safely behind bars by the time I'm done letting him know what I think about his behavior."

"You'd be surprised by how many people don't pay taxes." She ran her fingers through his hair. "They think that they earned the money, and it should be theirs to keep. Even people who have millions just think they can keep silent about it on their returns and nothing will happen. Yet they're still driving on roads and sending their kids to schools paid for by our taxes."

"Human nature. It's a constant battle for some of us to pretend to be civilized." He winked. "And trust me, I don't pay any more taxes than I have to myself. It'd probably be part of your job to finesse that, as well."

"I've been doing that for much bigger corporations for years. Maybe I'd like to do something else."

"Like what?"

She bit her lip and thought for a minute. The idea was outrageous, but then so was everything else about being here. "I always wanted to teach. My parents told me that the schools are full of unteachable, rowdy hoodlums and that I'd be miserable, which is why I pursued a career with numbers, but sometimes I wonder if I made the wrong choice."

"Interesting." He peered at her. "Now that we are gathering tribal members from far and wide, we have a lot to teach them about the business. Maybe you could start there, then get your teaching credentials and branch out to teaching in the schools."

"I like that idea." Her mind was racing, which was funny since her body still hummed with the aftereffects of their lovemaking. "It would be nice to work with people instead of numbers for a change."

"I think you'll be great at it." He kissed her softly on her mouth.

"I'll resign tomorrow. I wonder if they'll make me work for a final two weeks, or if they'll escort me out the door with my possessions in a cardboard box."

His eyes twinkled. "Once they know you're marrying me, probably the latter."

She felt a grin spread across her face. "I guess that's a good thing, under the circumstances."

"It most certainly is."

Epilogue

Thanksgiving

"Some people say that Native Americans shouldn't celebrate Thanksgiving." John stood at the head of the crowded table in the dining room of their meticulously renovated farmhouse. The fine cherry table was laden with fresh local turkey, roasted corn, chestnuts, maple-glazed squash with walnuts and glistening cranberry sauce. "They say that it was a foolish mistake of our ancestors to show the Pilgrims how to eat and survive in our land. They think it would have been better to let them starve to death."

He paused and looked around at the gathered guests. His grandparents beamed proudly and Constance wondered if they'd heard this speech before. "I disagree. Every choice we make in life shapes who we become and I'm proud to be a descendant of those who chose to offer the hand of friendship. I prefer to hope for the best and that's how I live my life. Our people have certainly been through many trials and tribulations since then, but we're still here and we're looking forward to a vibrant future."

He raised his champagne flute, and Constance lifted hers. She still couldn't believe this tall, handsome man was her husband. "And that future has just grown a little bit brighter..." He glanced at her and she smiled back. They'd talked about when to make their announcement and decided this was the perfect time. She felt butterflies in her stomach, fluttering around the tiny baby growing there.

"Because we're expecting a new member of the Nissequot tribe, who should be joining us sometime in June."

His grandmother gasped and turned to her husband. "A baby? Oh, John, did you hear that?"

"I heard it." He beamed and patted her hand. "That's wonderful."

The round of congratulations made Constance blush, and a sudden rush of emotion propelled her to her feet. A hush fell over the room as she looked around, feeling such a strong connection to the people gathered there. "These last few months have been a whirlwind. In May I was still living quietly in my childhood bedroom in Ohio, in June I got the assignment that would bring me here for the first time and now, in November, I'm an expectant mother, married to an amazing man, living in a lovely farmhouse in Massachusetts and pursuing a teaching license. I'm still a bit shell-shocked by it all, but I'm so grateful for the way you've all welcomed me into your midst and made my transition to my new life so easy and enjoyable."

Even her parents were smiling. They'd driven up here for the wedding, and now for Thanksgiving, and John's relentlessly charming grandfather had taken over the task of winning their hearts for the Nissequot tribe and casino. Although he still had a way to go, he'd made impressive progress.

John raised his glass. "I already find it hard to remember what life was like before you came here. Every day I'm grateful for the BIA investigation that brought you into our lives." A chuckle rumbled around the room. "Even Don says he's glad Constance caught up with him before he dug himself into an even deeper hole. He's lucky to have got off with only a six-week sentence."

The casino had shrugged off the scandal and the publicity from it brought in more people than ever, so New

Dawn was growing from strength to strength. "Next year we should be able to complete the purchase of seven hundred acres along our eastern border and break ground on the water park." Amusement twinkled in his eyes as he looked at Constance. The water park had been her idea. She liked the idea of expanding in a family-friendly direction and offering summer camps there for kids from all over the region. "Every day around here is a new adventure and I'm glad to be sharing them with my soul mate."

"I love you," she said softly.

"I love you, too, sweetheart." He spoke the words just to her, and emotion flowed directly between them despite all the people gathered around them. "And I'm thankful that I get to spend the rest of my life with you."

She felt tears well in her eyes and was about to blame the pregnancy hormones when she noticed that she wasn't the only one having that reaction. "Sometimes there's so much to be thankful for that it's hard to know where to start, so I suggest we all enjoy this delicious meal before it gets cold," she said.

John's grandfather chimed in. "I like the way you think. We give thanks to the Creator for this fine meal and the pleasure of sharing it together. Let's eat!"

* * * * *

COMING NEXT MONTH FROM

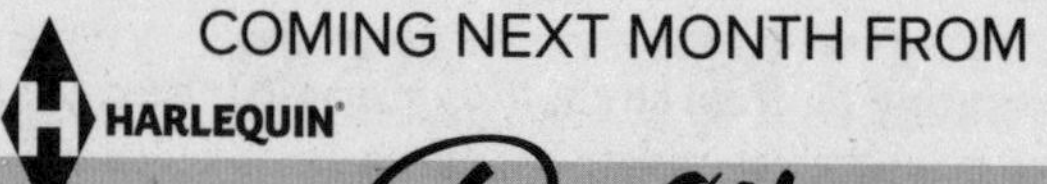

Desire

Available November 4, 2014

#2335 THE COWBOY'S PRIDE AND JOY
Billionaires and Babies • by Maureen Child
A wealthy rancher who loves his reclusive mountain, Jake never could resist Cassidy. Especially not when she introduces him to his infant son...just as a snowstorm forces them to face everything that's still between them...

#2336 SHELTERED BY THE MILLIONAIRE
Texas Cattleman's Club: After the Storm • by Catherine Mann
An unexpected passion ignites between single mom and conservationist Megan and her adversarial neighbor. But when she learns the real estate magnate threatens what she's trying to protect, she has to decide—trust the facts...or her heart?

#2337 FROM ENEMY'S DAUGHTER TO EXPECTANT BRIDE
The Billionaires of Black Castle • by Olivia Gates
Rafael Salazar is poised to destroy the man who stole his childhood, but his feelings for his enemy's daughter may threaten his plans. When she becomes pregnant, will he have to choose between revenge and love?

#2338 A BEAUMONT CHRISTMAS WEDDING
The Beaumont Heirs • by Sarah M. Anderson
As best man and a PR specialist, Matthew Beaumont needs his brother's Christmas wedding to be perfect. Then former wild child Whitney Maddox becomes a bridesmaid. Will she ruin the wedding? Or will Matthew discover the real woman behind the celebrity facade?

#2339 THE BOSS'S MISTLETOE MANEUVERS
by Linda Thomas-Sundstrom
Chad goes undercover at the agency he bought to oversee a Christmas campaign. But when the star ad exec with a strange aversion to the holiday jeopardizes the project, Chad doesn't know whether to fire her or seduce her!

#2340 HER DESERT KNIGHT
by Jennifer Lewis
The last thing Dani needs after her divorce is an affair with a man from the family that's been feuding with hers for decades. But notorious seducer Quasar may be the only man who can reawaken her body...and her heart.

YOU CAN FIND MORE INFORMATION ON UPCOMING HARLEQUIN® TITLES, FREE EXCERPTS AND MORE AT WWW.HARLEQUIN.COM.

HDCNM1014